I0669195

UNFAZED PUBLISHING
YOUR MIND IS OUR BUSINESS

KLARIZZA BAE

SOMETIMES

IT'S

GOOD

TO BE

BAD

UNFAZED PUBLISHING
YOUR MIND IS OUR BUSINESS

TAMPA FLORIDA

ISBN: 9781959275350

Library Of Congress Number: 2024908649

| Table Of Contents |

UNFAZED PUBLISHING
YOUR MIND IS OUR BUSINESS

www.UnfazedPublishing.com

Chapter One

| The Reunion |

(…Knock. Knock. Knock.) The door sounded.

"Yes. Who is it?" Tasha uttered.

"It's me Greg." He replied.

The door opens. "How ya been?" Greg said with open arms. "I'm just fine." Tasha answered with a big smile, "It has been a minute huh?" "Yes, it has been." Greg replied hugging her warmly. "But, you are getting younger and more beautiful by the day." He looked her right into her eyes. "You old charmer." Tasha responded. "You haven't changed have you?" "All I can tell you is that I missed you." Greg shared very sincerely. "How about a drink?" Tasha asked. "I would love that." Greg answered. "How's the family?" Tasha inquired. "They are doing fine." Greg replied.

In the kitchen they sat there drinking wine and catching up on everything. The conversation flowed so naturally like they never missed a beat. However, it had been about 10 years since they last saw each other. "I hope you don't mind. I ordered some wings from this new place." Tasha told him. "While they are being delivered, I'm going to make you my super-duper orange frozen daiquiri. It's to die for; trust me. If you don't like it you can get your money back." "Hmmm, nothing beats a money back guarantee." Greg chuckled. "I'll try anything once."

The wings were fall off the bone good and the daiquiri was potent yet surprisingly tasty as promised. Time flew by and it was getting late. Greg being a gentleman told Tasha that he had to go. Tasha did not want to hear it. "Look…, you have had a lot to drink." Tasha stated. "It's not worth a DUI or an accident. You have had several glasses of wine and a couple of daquiris. You can crash here until the morning. I insist." "You sure?" Greg asked. "Yes. You can sleep on the couch." Tasha replied. "I'll get you some pillows, and a comfortable blanket. You will sleep like a baby." Tasha then explained to Greg how to work the TV. She gave him access to the bathroom and to anything he wanted in the fridge. She also gave him access to her computer in case he wanted to play chess online, surf the internet, or whatever. She was a generous and gracious host.

Tasha went to her room and Greg stretched out on the couch. He thought to himself that he wanted to cook breakfast for Tasha the next morning. He wanted to check with her to see what she would like for breakfast, so he went to her room. The door was open and he asked, "Are you decent?" Nonetheless, she didn't hear him. She was in the shower. Greg could see her from the doorway. Her silhouette was clearly visible through the shower door. He caught himself staring for a moment or two. He thought to himself, "My, my, my. When God made Tasha, He threw away the mold." Not wanting to get caught, he went back to the living room and got back into his bed. As Tasha exited the shower, she saw him going back to the living room. She came out wrapped in a light blue towel. "Did you need something? Everything ok?" "Yeah…, everything is fine." Greg responded. "I just wanted to know what you would like for breakfast. I want to cook for you in the morning." "You love to cook don't you?" Tasha uttered with a big smile. "Well, I'd like French toast and sausage. I'd like my eggs scrambled with cheese and seasoned with Rosemary. And I'd like salsa with my eggs too." "You got it." Greg released with confidence. There was sexual tension there, but Greg was on his best behavior despite the fact that he was aroused. Tasha was completely comfortable around Greg. She really trusted him. She felt a little bit daring that evening. Maybe it was the wine or the daquiris that were kicking in. Therefore, she went back to her room and put on her favorite pink babydoll see-thru lingerie. It barely covered her curvy figure. She just wanted to get a little rise out of Greg. She was in a playful mood and wasn't sleepy at all. She said to herself, 'Sometimes it's good to be bad.' Tasha walked to the kitchen, but she deliberately went in front of the couch between Greg and the TV so he would notice her sexy pink outfit. "Wow!" Greg sighed. "Heaven must be missing an angel." "I love that song." Tasha stated enthusiastically. "You want me to play some music?" "Sure." "You remember this old one?" Tasha asked. She played 'Slow Jam' by Midnight Star. "Oh yeah," Greg replied. "Would you like to dance?"

Greg wanted Tasha and Tasha wanted Greg. She looked stunning in her see-thru lingerie. It was truly a struggle for Greg to keep his eyes on her face. The outfit was very short displaying her beautifully shaped legs. The two of them were all alone staring into each other's eyes as their bodies drew closer together. Greg's arms wrapped around her slender waist. Tasha placed her hands on his muscular chest. She could feel her heart beating stronger and stronger. He was finally holding his sexy angel in his arms. Perfect! It was a very romantic scene that was about to heat up even more. It had been a while since Tasha had slow danced with anyone; especially with a man she secretly had a crush on. "What does this song remind you of?" Greg smiled and replied, "The first time I walked you home from school and we shared our first kiss." Greg caressed Tasha's face in his hands and paused. Tasha's heart felt like it stopped as butterflies overwhelmed her stomach. She knew what was coming next. 'What is this guy doing to me?' She thought to herself.

Finally their lips slowly pressed together. It was a very tender and passionate kiss. She soon felt his full tongue thrusting beyond her wet lips, swirling erotically inside of her mouth. Greg savored the taste of Tasha's sweet lips. The stimulation of Greg's kiss set off a spasm of electricity in Tasha's lower body. Tasha knew at this moment she wanted to feel Greg's strong love deep inside her. After sharing this intimate sensuous kiss, Greg drew back and stared at her intensely. Tasha was made weak gazing at his stare. Another song started to play as they held each other gently. It was Cheryl Lynn and Luther Vandross's hit, "If This World Was Mine." Tasha managed to unhook the top part of her babydoll lingerie on the sly as they embraced and started back slow dancing. She suddenly took it off and tossed it on the couch so smoothly. You would have thought she was accustomed to being topless in front of Greg which was not the case at all. Being surprised, Greg muttered under his breath, "OMG." The slow danced ended. It was time for Greg to take Tasha, his sexy angel, to heaven. He wanted to impress her and delight her at the same time. He said, "Wait here for a second," as he sat her down on the couch. The song continued playing softly in the background. He quickly dashed into the bathroom where he remembered seeing some coconut oil, and a couple of little bottles of essential oils. He grabbed them and returned swiftly. "Lay back and relax Baby." His hands felt like warm reoccurring waves of the ocean as he spread the oils on her soft naked skin. With each stroke of his hands, the passion of intense desire began to rise in Tasha. "Ohhh yes that fells so good baby." she whispered. She loved being pampered. She loved being the center of Greg's attention. She was captivated by Greg's affectionate care. He was spoiling her which is something he loved to do. In her mind, he was perfect for her. He understood her. She trusted him completely and he listened to her. Yes, this was fast, but when you know it's real love, you just know.

Greg was spreading the fragrant oils over her ample breasts with a tenderness, and the precision of a conductor of an orchestra playing the most enchanting melody. A reoccurring theme which keeps building and building to a sexual crescendo. Tasha was about to explode. She was ready and willing to make the most intimate connection between a man and woman. She had arrived. She wanted Greg, but Greg was still taking his sweet time. He wanted to go beyond pleasing Tasha; if there is such a thing. He wanted her to never forget the first time they made love. It had to be special. You don't get a second chance at the first time, but Tasha had other plans. No more waiting, longing, and languishing in this red-hot passion to connect intimately. She made a subtle move of her hand sliding it up the inside of his leg. "Hmmm," Greg said a bit caught off guard by the fact that Tasha was making her move when he was the one calling the shots. "Mmmm," he said as she held his tool in her warm hand. Greg lost his place for a second. Now the pleaser had become the one being pleased. He paused to catch his breath. She continued her targeted massage as she rose from the couch. She gently grabbed the head of his Johnson with 3 fingers. She tugged at it pulling him in the direction of her bedroom. He followed like a dog on a leash. Greg's eyes were intently focused on her glorious booty as it gyrated with each step she took towards the bedroom. It was perfectly shaped and it was no secret that Greg was a booty man. Don't get it twisted he loved breasts too, but in a pinch if he had to make a choice, he would take the booty hands down. Tasha had tiny pink panties on. Greg was calculating how to remove them quickly. When she got to the bed and turned towards him, Greg pulled the panties down in one quick swoop. She giggled as she willingly stepped out of them. Now Greg's mission was complete. He had a perfectly shaped, beautiful, sexy, naked woman primed for passionate intimacy. He told Tasha, "I hope you are ready for this." She smiled and replied, "You're the one I hope is ready for this." They both laughed as their dance began.

It was exactly 1:35am. As the music played softly in the

background, the aroused lover's hearts were beating in harmony. Greg pulled Tasha closer to him while they were still standing and he could smell the tangerine body spray she was wearing. He imagined that her nectar would taste as sweet as the flavor of tangerine juice. "Tasha…" Greg said getting her attention because she was lost in the moment. Greg caressed her beautiful face in his hands and looked deep into her light brown eyes. He explained, "…I want this to be our special moment together. I want us to never forget what we do and say this night." Tears started welling up in Tasha's eyes, "Yes me too, and Greg, don't forget that I'm giving you my everything. Don't ever forget the love that I'm giving you tonight. It is all that you will ever need. I feel that you are perfect for me and I am perfect for you. Just promise me that you will never give up on our love no matter what happens."

Greg laid her down gently on the bed and he began to kiss her body starting with the toes then kissing up her leg. He kissed his way up her thighs until he reached the warm sweetness of the lips of her tenderness. "Mmmmmm… Uhhhhhh…" Tasha moaned in a whisper. Greg continued to delight her as Tasha's back began to arch as she squirmed with passionate pleasure. She grabbed Greg's head pulling him closer as she began to climax. "Don't stop Greg…" Tasha pleaded. "…this feels soooo good." Greg was encouraged by Tasha's words. He just wanted to make this first time memorable. Therefore, he continued to please Tasha intimately; even more vigorously. Now the time had come for Greg to connect with his angel. He positioned himself to enter her while she was on her back. As he penetrated her, he began to promise that he would never ever give up on their love no matter what. Yet, he wasn't satisfied so he began to thrust his cock into her in a rhythmic fashion articulating, "I … will … never … give … up … on … this … love." in perfect rhythm with his penetrations. He was literally driving the point home so she would never forget it.

Greg was completely committed to Tasha and Tasha to Greg. Tasha changed her position. She had Greg sit up with his back against the headboard and straddled him. Allowing his strong erect male organ slide inside her. She wanted that intimate connection with him. She bounced up and down on him for a while. Her titties were dancing in sync. She was having a good time. Greg was hanging on for dear life with his arms around her. She slowed down and began working his equipment back and forth. "Oh my God. That feels so good." Greg moaned. "I just want you to know that I heard your promise, and I make the same promise to you." Tasha says in a sexy undertone while riding Greg cowgirl style. She began rhythmically working her hips back and forth telling him, "I … will … never … give … up … on … this … love." These were unforgettable moments for Greg and Tasha. The couple was off to a great start. Greg had one more treat for his angel. Greg positioned Tasha on her back slowly entering her, sliding it in as deep as he could. His penetrations were slow, deliberate, and consistent. Sometimes he went up and down, then changed his movement working it round and round, but the main thing was Greg's pace. He went slow and didn't increase his speed. Tasha loved it. She couldn't resist complimenting him because she wanted him to do that to her every time. "Baby, I love that." She uttered breathlessly. "I love the way you work it slowly." Tasha was in heaven and she would never forget this night. It was special for both of these inspired lovers. This couple had the most memorable night of love making just like Greg wanted. They were finally together and nothing could separate them. Greg was totally satisfied with Tasha and she was completely satisfied with her man Greg. What could possibly go wrong?

Chapter Two
|Tasha's Friend|

Greg went to Tasha's job because he had a scheduled lunch date with her. Her job was on the third floor. The receptionist notified Tasha she had a visitor and she asked, "Could you please send him up? I have a report that I need to send off before I go." "No problem." Tiffany (The Receptionist) replied. She informed Greg, "Sir. You can go to the third floor and take a left when you come out the elevator." "Thank you." Greg smiled. It was his first time at Tasha's job. As he got off the elevator he went to the left and he saw his angel. He walked over to her and gave her a kiss, "How are you baby?" "I'm fine," She answered, "Can you wait here at my desk for me a few minutes I got to send out this report?" "Absolutely. No problem." Greg responded. Tasha hurried off.

"Hmmm…, so you're Greg." A voice uttered from the next desk. "Yeah, guilty as charged." Greg joked as he turned to see who was speaking to him. "And who pray tell are you, if you don't mind me asking?" "I am Tasha's friend." Said the strikingly beautiful woman. "Ok. Does her good friend have a name?" Greg asked playfully. "My name is Cynthia." She replied. "Very pleased to make your acquaintance Cynthia." Greg responded. "So…, I finally meet Mr. Perfect." Cynthia announced. "You know it's an oxymoron: 'A Perfect Man.'" "Yeah, I get it." Greg responded, "No one is perfect, but I love my girl and it has been a whirlwind romance for us both.

I can truly say that Tasha is perfect for me too." "Wow, you two are really in love." Cynthia replied, "and that is beautiful. I shouldn't be so cynical. I got to work on that." "So…, Cynthia…, where are you from?" Greg asked. "I'm from all over." Cynthia answered, "I was an army brat. My dad and mom were both in the military. We moved from place to place. I lived for a time in LA and we lived for a while in Tampa Bay, FL. Also, we lived in Arlington, Virgina. I'm pretty well rounded because of it, but it was hard to keep friends because we were constantly moving." "Yeah, I know the drill," Greg stated, "but you have turned out well. So, what brings you to Hotlanta?" "Well, I love the climate and there is so much culture here." Cynthia shared, "This is a happening place." "Yes, it is." Greg agreed. At that moment Tasha returned. "Ahh, I see you met my friend Cynthia." Tasha said. "Yep," Greg responded, "pleased to have met you Cynthia. May God bless you. See ya later." Tasha and Greg headed off to lunch while Cynthia watched them leave the floor before getting back to work.

Greg is a busy guy. He is chasing after that dollar. After Greg gets off from work, he has his own business that he does. He runs a food truck selling meals and barbeque wings. Therefore, he is always preparing food and running to the store to buy meat, rice, beans, potatoes and any other thing needed to run his food truck. Actually, he does well because he is a talented cook. He works hard and everyone loves his food. He is saving his money to take Tasha to Vegas. It is a surprise. Now Tasha understands that he doesn't have a lot of free time. She mainly sees him on Friday night,

Saturday night, and all day Sunday. She is ok with this, but she does miss her man.

At Tasha's job, all the girls were buzzing about this latest women's magazine article entitled, "Does your man want a Menage a trois? Cynthia drops the magazine on Tasha's desk. "Check out the article on page 5." Cynthia suggested. "Ok girl," Tasha replied, "I'll read it during my lunch." "Get back with me on it." Cynthia declared, "I'm dying to hear your thoughts." Meanwhile, Greg was excited he discovered a new thing to make for dessert. He named it a "Piecaken." He was trying to explain it to Tasha over the phone. "No, it's simple," Greg explained, "you bake a pie, like say a sweet potato pie. Then you bake another pie, like say a pecan pie. Then you bake a cake like an apple spice cake. Then you put one pie on the bottom and cover it with icing. The next pie on top of that to form the 2nd layer and put icing on that. Then add the apple spice cake on top and cover the top of the cake with apple pie filling. OMG!" "Baby that sounds like sugar overload." Tasha said. "Ok, no doubt," Greg admitted, "but these things are selling like hot cakes. It has become very popular here in Atlanta in recent times. I could easily sell one for forty bucks. I tell you what, I'm gonna make one for you to taste." "Ok, I'll taste it Greg, but don't leave that cake at my house. A girl has got to watch her figure. Ok? Babe I got to get back to work. I love you, and will see you later. Call me. Bye Boo." "Bye Babe." Greg replied. Cynthia was right there when Tasha got off the phone. She asked, "What did ya think about the article?" Tasha just laughed. "Oh, I know what you're gonna say." Cynthia responded, "That's crazy! Who would do that with their man? Not me. Am I right?" "Come on Cynthia." Tasha protested, "Would you let your man, that you love, screw another woman right in front of you? No, I'm serious. Answer me girl." Tasha said passionately. "Well Tasha, don't knock it until you tried it." Cynthia responded. "You've done this before haven't you?" Tasha asked in disbelief. "Mmmm, not exactly." Cynthia replied with a bit of hesitation, "It wasn't my boyfriend. I was the third wheel." "Really?!" Tasha was stunned. "How was it girl? Do tell." "Well, from my point of view, it was harmless." Cynthia explained, "I mean you know the dude very well. My girlfriend talked about him all the time. So, you knew exactly what kind of man you were going to sleep with. I knew stuff about him that I don't think he knew about himself. His girlfriend told me everything down to his sexual tendencies, his fears, his fantasies, his greatest pleasure, and his biggest weakness. I went into the situation well informed and well prepared." "And she was ok with you sleeping with her man?" Tasha asked. "Yeah, she was present of course." Cynthia said, "She learned more about her man in that night than the entire time she was dating him; believe it or not. And furthermore, they both had a blast. It was a moment that they will treasure together forever." Really? Come on Cynt." Tasha blurted out with skepticism, "How could letting another woman sleep with your man be fun?" "We just let ourselves go," Cynthia explained, "we had fun picking out our sexy outfits. We challenged him with various positions and sexual techniques. We played games like how fast can you make him cum? Or, can you make her orgasm? We took him to the strip club to find out what kind of woman he was most attracted to. It was good fun and we really pushed him to his limit. It was two of us and one of him. We had the advantage every time. My girlfriend learned how to please him better and discovered a few things that she wasn't doing in bed that he absolutely loved. When you know what a man craves and what he loves, then you can become that on command. It gives you real power in your relationship." "Hmmm, I don't know." Tasha was perplexed thinking deeply, "Do you recommend it since you experienced it? Is it something that you would do?" "Listen to me Tasha…," Cynthia explained, "you should do what you want to do. You should find out what he wants to do. I know that you respect marriage so if you are going to do this, do it before you get married. You should know what he likes and what turns him on sexually. No, I mean what turns him on all the way!" "Hmmm, you got me thinking about this." Tasha admitted slowly. "Have you ever taken him to a strip club?" Cynthia asked in a challenging manner. She knew that Tasha was a church girl and would never frequent a place like that. "Do you even know what kind of girls he finds attractive? Hispanics girls, black girls, white girls, light skinned women? How about him? Does he know what kind of man turns you on?" "No, no and no. I don't know any of those things about him." Tasha confessed a little taken back. "I will not tell you what to do. You are a grown-ass woman Tasha…," Cynthia continued, "you take responsibility for yourself and your actions. But, include your man in this decision. Ask him if he has ever wanted to have a threesome. What could it hurt? I mean it's better to know now than to find out later. Right?" "Right." Tasha said in deep thought. It's clear that Cynthia is very persuasive. Cynthia studied psychology in college and has read every book that deals with sexual psychology. She is planting a seed in Tasha's mind, and she will patiently wait until that seed grows on its own. She needs this to be Tasha's idea not Cynthia's.

Greg is planning another surprise for Tasha. For her birthday, he wants to get her a wonderful gift that is practical. He wants to get her just what she wants, and just what she needs. Of course, he has no clue what that will be. In fact, he thinks that it might be several different things. Consequently, he came up with a great plan to find out exactly what Tasha needs. He would enlist the help of her friend Cynthia. Greg needed to talk to Cynthia without Tasha around. Easier said than done. If Greg could get Tasha to take a day off from work, then he could simply go to Tasha's job and speak to Cynthia without Tasha being present. Accordingly, Greg promised to spend a weekend with Tasha whenever she could get a Friday off. They planned on going around the city to see some sites and in the evening, Greg would prepare a wonderful meal for Tasha. Greg insisted on Tasha sleeping in on that Friday. The site seeing would start after 11am. That would give him the chance to go to Tasha's job and speak to Cynthia without Tasha being around. When the weekend arrived, Greg's plan worked to perfection. He got up that morning and went to Tasha's job to speak to Cynthia. The receptionist told him that Cynthia would be down shortly. "Hey Greg," Cynthia greeted him, "how are you? Is everything ok?" "Everything is just fine." Greg replied, "How are you?" "Good." Cynthia responded. "I came to ask you a favor," Greg began, "I want to surprise Tasha with a special gift, but I don't know what to get her. Could you help me find out exactly what Tasha needs? I will pay you for your time." "Ok, how do you want me to do this?" Cynthia asked. "Take her shopping with you one day after work. Take her to a variety of stores and see if there is anything that she really wants or really needs. Maybe she needs multiple things. If so, just let me know what you find out. Here is some money if you are willing to help me out with this." "Greg, I consider you a friend," Cynthia reminded him, "I will do this because I know that it will make Tasha so very happy. I don't want the money. This is a labor of love for you and my best friend." "Thank you so much Cynthia." Greg said with excitement, "I owe you. Please keep this between you and I so it will be a surprise for her, ok?" "Ok, but we need to be in touch," Cynthia told him. "Let me get your number and I will give you mine." "Cynthia, you are the best." Greg replied, "Don't forget that I owe you a huge favor. I always pay my debts so when there is something that I can do for you, don't you hesitate to ask me. God bless you. You are a true friend."

The seed Cynthia planted in the mind of Tasha was starting to grow on its own. Tasha was comfortable with the idea of doing a threesome before marriage. It would be like an experiment. Like an exploration that both her and Greg could enjoy together. She knew that Greg loved her completely and that there was a difference between sex and love. Thus, she made the decision to ask Greg about a threesome. She invited him over for breakfast one Saturday morning. After breakfast she spoke to him about it. "Ok. Let me get this straight." Greg clarified, "Not two guys and one girl, but two girls with one guy, right?" "Right." Tasha assured. "Yeah," Greg added, "I've thought about this before. I mean, what guy wouldn't like to be with two beautiful women. That is like the ultimate ego boost for any guy." "I don't care about other guys babe. I'm asking you is this something that you want?" "Hmmm, you know that I love you and only you." Greg confidently stated without hesitation, "I'm not going to risk losing everything I have with you pursuing my adolescent male ego. Baby, I'm not quite as dumb as I look." "No, this is not a trick question to see if you love me or not." Tasha replied, "I know you love me. What I'm asking you is do you want to explore this with me?" "I find it hard to believe that you want to do this." Greg alleged, "who would want their man to have sex with another beautiful woman? I mean, how could you possibly benefit from that arrangement?" "Good question." She replied, "I want to know everything about you, I want to know everything about your sexuality. What kind of girls turn you on? What gets your motor running in the bedroom? What things do you fear sexually? Are there things that I can do in the bedroom to please you better? And vice versa. Really, what do you know about me sexually? Do you know what type of guy turns me on?" "Well, no." Greg muttered slowly reflecting on what Tasha was saying, "I don't know any of those things about you." "Greg, I think this will be a chance for us to find out all these things together." Tasha expounded convinced that she was right. "We could have fun exploring this together. We could play games with it, challenge each other, and please each other to an extreme degree. When is the last time you've been in a strip club? When is the last time you went skinny dipping? Have you ever had two hotties on your arm and both of them crazy about you? We could have contests like how fast can you give me an orgasm, or give her an orgasm? How long can you keep from cumming while being stimulated by two sexy girls? Oh come on! You will really enjoy yourself baby. I guarantee it." "Clearly you have given this some deep thought." Greg responded, "Where did this idea come from? Honestly, where did you come up with the thought of a threesome? I've never heard you talk about it before." "The girls at work had been talking about it." She expressed, "There was this article in a woman's magazine about it." "Hmmm…, well baby…, you know… I will do anything for you," Greg started off slow. "I have always listened to you because I trust you. Right?" "Right." Tasha answered. "I'm a pretty open-minded guy." He continued, "My only concern is that we may destroy what we have here by trying this thing. I want you to understand that." "I understand." Tasha replied. "I belong to you Tasha." Greg passionately avowed, "I will do whatever it takes to please you. The only thing I ask is that we don't tear our relationship apart over this. I don't want to hear any regrets about doing this later. Agreed?" "Agreed." She lovingly confirmed. "If we are going to do this Tasha, it is totally up to you. I will trust you on this one." Greg was still blown away by this conversation. He couldn't stop thinking about this thing. Inside he was a bit worried, but he was also curious. The thought of having two beautiful girls was delicious to him though. The ball was in Tasha's hands.

The next day Tasha made a phone call. "Girl he said yes!" Tasha exclaimed with excitement in her voice. "Oh wow! Now what are you going to do?" Cynthia asked laughing. "I don't know." Tasha replied, "This is crazy. I'm in territory that I have never been in before. He left everything up to me and said he would trust my judgement. I can't blow this. I got to get it right." "Don't you worry." Cynthia reassured her, "I'm here with you every step of the way. Remember I've been through this before. I will help you navigate your way through this. This is the love of your life. The man that will become your husband. I know this is your soulmate so you can't take any unnecessary risks. Too much is at stake. Right?" "Oh yeah." Tasha responded, "That's for sure." "Do you have someone in mind to be the other woman?" Cynthia asked curiously. "No, I haven't gotten that far yet." Tasha answered. "Well, take your time." Cynthia encouraged her, "There is no rush. But make sure that you don't get some young inexperienced idealistic girl that can mess this whole thing up. You need an experienced, cultured, mature woman that you can trust with your most prized possession; your man. And she needs to be sexy enough to turn your man on." "I've got to be comfortable with her too." Tasha told her, "I would have to trust her completely." "Absolutely." Cynthia said, "We can talk about this some more on Tuesday when we go shopping together girl. Just know that I am here for you and for Greg to make sure this thing goes off without a hitch. So, you take your time in deciding who you trust to be this other woman."

The cell phone rang and after a couple of rings Cynthia answered, "Hello." "Hi, it's me Greg. How are you? Hope I didn't catch you at a bad time." "No, not at all." Cynthia responded, "How are you?" "Great. I'm checking in with you to see how the whole shopping thing went with Tasha." He answered. "It was great. Cynthia admitted, "We hung out, bonded, and talked about a certain guy named Greg. Otherwise known as Mr. Perfect." She laughed. "Reall? Is that so?" Greg joked, "Did my secret agent find out what Tasha wants or what she needs?" "Your secret agent did find out the information that you need." Cynthia confessed, "But I'm not gonna tell you over the phone. I want to go with you to buy it because I know the store, the brand, and the exact model that Tasha wants." "Ok. Is it just one item?" Greg asked. "No." Cynthia replied with a smile in her voice, "Tasha also wants to get rid of all of her colored towels in the house and replace them with white towels. Her skin is sensitive to the towels that have color in them. She needs to have all white towels, and I mean the super high-quality towels that are 30 percent larger than your regular towels." "I'm guessing that's not all." Greg responded, "There is something else isn't there?" "Hmmm..., you are quite intuitive." Cynthia shared somewhat impressed. "There is this beautiful diamond necklace that she has her eye on, but it is a bit out of her price range. Trust me, 'it is to die for' and Greg, this necklace will melt her heart. You will be her hero. No, you will be her superhero. So, how did your secret agent do?" "My secret agent exceeded my expectations." Greg boasted, "Cynthia you are the best! Now I will blow her away on her birthday. When can we go shopping for these items?" "Greg, I've been wanting to go to this new restaurant." Cynthia suggested with some excitement in her voice. "Do you think your secret agent did well enough to be taken out to this fancy restaurant by her boss?" "Without a doubt." Greg announced without hesitation. "How does Wednesday sound for you?" She asked. "Wednesday is perfect." Greg replied, "It's a date."

The plan was to meet up at Tasha's job about 15 mins after 5pm. That would allow everyone, including Tasha, to be gone. Greg arrived right on time. He went inside the building and saw Cynthia coming out of the bathroom. "Wow, you look great." Greg confessed. "I changed my clothes so I could be comfortable." Cynthia replied. She was wearing what looked like skin tight jeans and a very flattering red blouse. "Well, you can't go wrong with jeans." Greg expressed. "Actually Greg...," she details, "these are not jeans. They are made of that stretchy material and painted to look like jeans. They are quite comfortable though." "Mmmm, I see." Greg muttered a bit distracted. Cynthia said, "Here's the plan. We go to the mall, you buy all three of the items that Tasha wants/needs, and afterwards, we can go to that new restaurant I told you about." "As Jean Luc Picard would say, 'make it so'." Greg attempted to make a joke. They both laughed. After they finished shopping at the mall, they got in Greg's car and headed to the new restaurant. Cynthia was sufficiently impressed with Greg's desire to please Tasha. "That was a lot of coins you dropped today on your lady." Cynthia noted, "Most guys would have only gotten one of those three things." "I just want to make her happy." Greg admitted. "I like you a lot." She said and continued, "You are a really good guy. You two are perfect together." "Thank you. I really appreciate what you've done as my personal secret agent. You are a true friend. I see why Tasha trust you so much."

After they pulled into the parking lot of the restaurant, Cynthia told Greg that she needed to change first. She headed to the Ladie's Room with a garment bag she previously placed in the back of Greg's car. "I'll meet you at the hostess stand in the lobby when you're finished changing." Greg advised Cynthia. "Ok." She answered. Greg didn't take a seat as he waited for Cynthia to return. He enjoyed the pleasant ambiance the restaurant exhibited. Very nice décor, music, and upscale on every level. As Greg engulfed himself in the atmosphere of the restaurant, he turns…, "…Holy Moses Cynthia! What are you wearing!?" Greg blurted out in utter surprise. "You like?" Cynthia asked as she did a twirl for him and letting him see her from every angle. "Ummm, you look, ummm…" Greg was at a loss for words, "…you look amazing." "Thank you." Cynthia said with a very confident smile. Cynthia came out of the Ladie's Room wearing a sparkling white party dress. The dress was so short that it barely covered her bottom. This dress highlighted her long attractive legs. There were some black lights in the restaurant so the dress not only sparkled, but it had a glowing purple hue about it as well. Cynthia looked like a sexy sparkling angel and that caught Greg totally off guard. Needless to say, she also caught the attention of many people in the restaurant. Greg and Cynthia enjoyed the new restaurant tremendously. (Cynthia pic below.)

After their meal Greg took Cynthia back to her car. Cynthia called Tasha later that night. "Hey. How is the search for the other woman going?" Cynthia asked. "Well, I got it narrowed down to 3

names." Tasha said. "Ok, who are these 3 people?" Cynthia asked. "Sarah Blake, Lisa Reyes, and Cynthia Heart." Tasha revealed. "Well, Lisa Reyes is married," Cynthia pointed out, " and her husband is in the military. He is stationed overseas. That's why you didn't know she was married." "Now it's down to two people." Tasha reasoned. "Tasha, it's your choice," Cynthia said, "Sarah is young. She's 23 or 24 years old. I'm totally willing to be the other woman, but again it's your choice." "Hypothetical here," Tasha asked, "let's say I chose you, what would be the next step?" "The next step is for three people to get to know each other," Cynthia confessed without hesitation, "Everyone has to agree to do this. You may be ok with me, but if Greg isn't ok with me it won't work. And conversely, if I am not ok with you, or with him, this will not work." "Do you want to do it?" Tasha asked. "Yeah," Cynthia replied without hesitation, "I trust you and I think that Greg is a quality guy." "You got the job Cynthia." Tasha announced, "I don't know Sarah and I don't feel good about her being with my man." "The biggest problem is going to be feeling left out," Cynthia explained, "no one wants to feel left out. Greg can only make love to one of us at a time, and it will be difficult to split the time perfectly every time we get together." "How do you address that problem?" Tasha asked. "Not easy, there is no easy solution," Cynthia said, "we have to manage it ourselves to the best of our abilities. We cannot let hurt feelings linger. If you feel slighted speak up, don't let it go, don't let it fester, and build up to an explosion. You keep an eye on me and I will keep an eye on you. Have you set a date?" "I'm thinking we should do this on Fridays so that we don't have anywhere to be the next morning." Tasha answered. "No, I haven't set a date yet, but soon." "Well, I think that we all need to meet up and spend some time together," Cynthia pointed out, "we need to make sure that we are all compatible and in agreement on doing this. We don't know for sure that Greg is attracted to me. I find him to be a handsome and charming man." "How's Wednesday for you?" Tasha asked. "That's fine for me." "Ok after work, you can come over to my place and we will have a meal together, sit, and talk afterwards." Tasha said.

"Sounds great," Cynthia replied, "but you and I need to have frequent meetings about this because Greg may not be comfortable being with another woman in front of you; initially. So you, and I, have to manage this situation until he feels free to enjoy both of us without reservation. You play the biggest role in this. Only you can give him permission to enjoy being with me. You must trust me and I must trust you for this to work." "I get it," Tasha reasoned, "you will need to be given time alone with him and time in front of me with him." "I'm the outsider," Cynthia explained, "I need to assert myself without pushing you out of the picture. We have to tag team this. There has to be communication between us frequently so we know where we are and we know where Greg is." "Now I need to talk to Greg," Tasha uttered slowly, "he needs to know that we are on for the threesome, and Wednesday is the day he will meet the woman that I have chosen to join us. I'm getting butterflies." Tasha was thinking of different ways that she could tell him about Wednesday. So, she called him and asked could he come over on Monday after his second job. He said, "Of course." When he arrived at her place he spoke with her. "Are you good? Is everything ok?" Greg asked. "I am wonderful. How are you?" She replied. "I doing fine." He answered. "I have some good news for you." Tasha announced, "We are going to have some fun this week." "What are you talking about?" Greg questioned looking very interested in her response. "I found someone who is perfect for a threesome." Tasha continued, "She is coming over Wednesday to meet you. We will have a meal with her and then we will talk about Friday night." "Friday night?" He asked. "If you are ok with this beautiful woman who I have selected for us," Tasha said hesitating and drawing out the words slowly, "Friday will be the first night of our threesome journey. I hope you are ready." "You know who it is, but you're not going to tell me." Greg guessed with a half-smile. "That's right buddy." Tasha responded, "You got to be there on Wednesday after work to find out in person. The suspense is killing you. Don't worry, we are going to have fun, and you are going to love her."

Chapter Three
| Cynthia's Heart |

Tuesday was the longest day of the year for Greg. He was nervously thinking would he like this woman and would he be able to make love to another woman in front of his beloved angel? If so, how would it be? Would it be strong passionate love or a weak passive intimate encounter? Would he embarrass himself? Doubts were running through his head all day. The doorbell rang. Tasha and Greg were in the kitchen. Tasha turned to her man and told him, "Go get the door and let your new friend in." Tasha was smiling from ear to ear. Greg went to the door and opened it. He immediately started laughing out of shock. He invited Cynthia in, "Welcome to Tasha's humble abode Cynthia." Cynthia was dressed like she was going to a business meeting. She was wearing a suit jacket and a skirt down to her knees. Greg was a bit confused. He would've guessed that she would be wearing something more strikingly sexy. Tasha came running from the kitchen to greet her dear friend. They were like 2 peas in a pod which kinda made Greg feel like the third wheel. The threesome enjoyed a nice dinner and a glass of wine. They took the party to the living room. "In order for this to work, there can be no secrets between us three," Cynthia explained, "we must develop trust and unity while having fun and exploring our fantasies. We can't leave anyone out. And Greg, we got to loosen you up so that you can be yourself in front of your lady." "Ahhh…, yeah, I could see that being a problem." Greg admitted. "Do you think you will be ok with me?" Cynthia asked rather direct. "I got no problem with you," Greg confessed, "I find you attractive." "Are you comfortable with me?" Cynthia asked as she stood up and started approaching Greg. "Yeah." Greg stated nervously getting more and more uncomfortable as Cynthia approached getting closer to him. Cynthia pulled off her jacket revealing a thin white tube top clinging to her breasts very tightly. Tasha came over and got the jacket from Cynthia. Greg realized this had been planned ahead of time. It was going off too smoothly. Then Cynthia dropped her knee-high skirt to the floor and stepped out of it. She was wearing a very short, tight sparkling red skirt. Again, like clockwork, Tasha grabbed the skirt off the floor and said, "Let me get this for you." Now he could see the entire shooting match: the long legs, the flat stomach, and the big breasts with no bra. Needless to say, her nipples were poking through the tube top. At this moment Greg became hard and had to make an adjustment. "Am I making you nervous?" Cynthia asked smiling. She was leaning over him as he sat on the couch. Her titties were dancing right in his face. They could hear each other's heartbeat they were so close. "No, not really." Greg answered. "There can be no secrets between us Greg." Cynthia repeated what she had told him earlier. "I'm good." he replied. "We love you if you are nervous. We love you if you are not nervous," Cynthia reasoned, "and we accept you as you are. Does this make you a little nervous?" Greg could smell her perfume she was so close to him. "A little," Greg admitted, "maybe a little." "Thank you for your honesty," Cynthia responded, "now please tell me why." "My girlfriend is right here with us now," Greg pointed out, "I do not want to cheat on her, or disrespect her." "A little help here Tasha," Cynthia called to her co-pilot. "Baby, we are going to have some fun," Tasha explained, "I give you my permission to enjoy yourself with Cynthia. Pretend she is your new girlfriend, and you are trying to get some off her. Play that game with her. How would you proceed. She is your prey and you are the hunter. Don't let her get away. I'm allowing you to do this with Cynthia. Do you find her desirable, attractive, captivating, and sexy? Then relax and go for it in front of me." "Friday, right?" Greg asked. "Yeah, Friday," Tasha responded. "Ok, I will be ready Friday." Greg announced confidently.

Greg found Cynthia attractive, but he just doesn't want to show that to Tasha. Friday was coming really, really fast. Thursday lasted for about 15 mins and it was Friday, just like that. Greg came up with a plan that would at least get him through this first Friday. He would make love to Tasha first, then he would ask Cynthia if she would role play with him. He wanted her to pretend to be Tasha so he could pretend to be having sex with Tasha, while he was intimate with Cynthia. Cynthia went for it, basically letting him off the hook. On that night, he made love to Cynthia just like he made love to Tasha. Greg's favorite outfit on Tasha was an orange colored see thru lingerie.

Tasha is a beautiful girl with light brown eyes. Her brown eyes go perfectly with the orange-colored lingerie outfit. She wore it for him often. He asked her to put it on that night. Greg always started out arousing his lady by softly licking and sucking her clit until she couldn't stand it anymore. Then he would start penetrating her, but he took his time when he made love to Tasha. Tasha affectionately called it, "slow dick." And she loved it. He would go slow and be very deliberate. Now Greg was doing the very same thing to Cynthia. He asked Cynthia to wear the orange lingerie outfit that Tasha always wore. It fit differently on Cynthia because she was taller than Tasha standing at 5ft 8'. Tasha was 5ft 5'. Cynthia understood the psychological explanation for it, but she figured she'd break him in slowly. Having some sex is better than none, or it is better than an embarrassed guy that is being humiliated. Cynthia was patient. She would break him down little by little. She had to admit that she did enjoy Greg's "slow dick." But, she wanted more from him, and most of all, she isn't Tasha. Greg has to learn how to love both of these completely different women in two completely different ways.

After the first Friday as a threesome, it was evident that Greg was not really having fun. Cynthia spoke to Tasha about it. "I don't think he really enjoyed himself," Cynthia said to Tasha, "he seemed to want to just get thru it, and get it over with. Did you notice that?" "Yeah," Tasha replied, "So what do we do about it? How do we help him relax and enjoy the sex?" "It is a process," Cynthia answered, "let me have him alone for a little while. Let's change things up on him. Let me go first and you leave the room. I will see if I can bring the real Greg out in the open. We won't let him pull that same trick of me pretending to be you again. We will insist that he make love to you, and he make love to me. Tasha we got to pull out all the stops on this one, because if we don't get him to come around, this threesome is over. I will call you and we will make sure this thing goes down without a hitch. We will perfect our plan." "Ok." Tasha responded fully on board.

The next Friday rolled around pretty quickly. Greg was not so uptight. He thought he was gonna pull the same stunt he did last week, but he is in for a rude awakening. Still, he can handle it. "I wondered where is Cynthia?" Greg noticed, "It's not like her to be late." "Hmmm, are you anxious to get started?" Tasha said jokingly. "Ha, ha. I'm just concerned if everything is ok with her." Greg stated. "No worries. She will be here in a minute," Tasha reassured him. "Cool." Greg replied. "We are going to change the lingerie tonight," Tasha explained, "in fact, babe we are going to change a few things tonight. We just want you to relax a little bit more, ok?" "O...k..." Greg muttered slowly. He was starting to get a little nervous because he realized that his plan wasn't going to work tonight. "I want Cynthia to explain it to you," Tasha declared, "she called. She's running a little late cause she picked up a special outfit just for you." "Really?" "Yes, really." Tasha replied. "Babe, can you open up a little bit more to her? I don't want her to feel like a third wheel. I realize that she is a little more aggressive than I am. That might be difficult for you to deal with, but I know you can handle her. You are a strong man and I know you can make her feel good. You are very loving and attentive. I want you to think of her like a new girlfriend - make her feel special – make her feel loved." Inside of his mind, Greg was really warming up to Cynthia. However, he didn't want Tasha to know. He learned a little bit last Friday concerning how to please Cynthia in bed. He feels like he needs more time with her to be better at pleasing her sexually.

When Cynthia arrived at Tasha's place, she was carrying a stylish little bag from a local lingerie shop. She entered the house and went straight up to Greg, looked him in the eye, and slowly leaned in to kiss him. It was a slow tender kiss which caught Greg off guard, but it had a calming effect on him. It was like a new girlfriend giving you a reassuring kiss early in the relationship. She stepped back while maintaining eye contact, and stated quite clearly, "Honey, I missed you." Greg felt funny saying it back to her, but he did, "Yeah.., ummm…., I missed you too." He said it in a very awkward way. "Sit down for a minute with us," Cynthia encouraged him, "we want to tell you something exciting." They all sat down in the living room. Cynthia started out by saying, "We are doing this threesome thing to have some fun and to learn more about each other. So, to help you relax and enjoy yourself tonight, we are going to do things a little differently." "Ok." Greg replied paying very close attention. "Tasha and I have decided to give you some time alone with me." Cynthia clarified staring intently at Greg's face to see his reaction. You could see the wheels in Greg's mind turning. He was trying to figure out what she meant. "So Tasha, are you good with this?" Greg asked. "I trust you and I trust Cynthia," Tasha replied confidently, "I don't have to be present when you make love to her. I've already given you my permission Greg, what more do you need?" "Tasha is a special girl and she deserves to be loved in a special way," Cynthia reminded him, "Right Greg?" "Right." Greg answered. "In time you will find that I, Cynthia Heart, I am very special also…," Greg interrupted her and finished the thought, "…And you deserved to be loved in a unique and special way as well. So, you don't have to pretend to be Tasha anymore. I get it. I get it." "Good. Now I have a little surprise for you in this bag," Cynthia said with a very big smile, "I'll be back." "Just relax and be yourself." Tasha encouraged Greg, "She'll be out in a minute." Tasha left the room for a moment heading to the kitchen.

After going to the bedroom Cynthia entered, Greg sat on the bed in silent anticipation. Tasha returned and entered the same bathroom with something in her hand. Greg couldn't make it out. Tasha purposely kept it out of his line of sight. One moment later, the two emerged from the bathroom. Tasha came out first and announced, "Greg, I give you your luscious, delectable dessert for the evening!" Tasha stepped to the side allowing this beautiful girl to come into view. "Oh my, my, my!" Greg exclaimed as he laid eyes on his tasty treat for this evening. Cynthia walked slowly towards Greg. She was a different person. She was shy. Like she was unsure of her stunning body. Unsure if he would be taken in by her natural beauty. She was wearing a bright red laced lingerie which did not cover her tender breasts. It was a crotchless outfit leaving nothing to the imagination. Now Tasha, while in the bathroom, added her touch to the outfit by placing a dallop of whipped cream over each nipple and a line of whipped cream over Cynthia's pussy. "Greg, enjoy your sweet dessert." Tasha encouraged him with a wicked smile as she left the room. Well, she didn't really leave completely. She hid around the corner just out of view of the lovely couple. She couldn't leave. There was too much riding on this sexual encounter. Cynthia was the only hope to save this threesome. Cynthia is the master at sexual psychology. If anyone could manipulate a man into feeling more comfortable, feeling more-free to have sex, and have fun in this threesome, it would be Cynthia. Tasha had to know if Cynthia would be successful tonight, so she sat quietly by the half-opened door listening intently.

Cynthia was radiant. She could feel her heart pounding. She was actually nervous and unsure if she could pull off this task. Cynthia was standing there before Greg who was sitting on the edge of the bed. "Hello Greg," she uttered sweetly, "I'm Delicious, pleased to meet you." Pretending as if they were meeting for the very first time. Maybe they were in Greg's mind. This was a new beginning. Greg laughed which helped him relax a little bit more. "Could you taste me to make sure I'm really Delicious?" "Don't mind if I do." Greg responded playfully. Greg stood up and gently placed his hands on the waist of Cynthia. He pulled her closer so he could lick the whipped cream off her breasts; one at a time. Greg began to suck her nipples while squeezing her breasts tenderly. "Oh yeah baby," Greg whispered, "you are definitely Delicious." "Wait sir, you're not done," She replied innocently. "I'm nothing if I'm not thorough." He said quietly as he began to kiss down her warm body. First the neck, then the chest, between the breasts, the stomach . . . "You're are getting closer," Cynthia whispered as her breathing suddenly got deeper and more frequent. Then she began to moan with pleasure as Greg gently enjoyed her sweet deliciousness with his warm wet tongue. He was in no rush and Cynthia was being aroused beyond what she had expected so early in this encounter. She did not want to be distracted. She was on a mission. She had a detailed plan that Tasha helped her draw up. After a few moments of unforgettable tantalizing pleasure, Cynthia pulled Greg up so that he was standing on his feet. She put her arms around him and began kissing him passionately. Greg was thinking to himself, 'What is this flavor? It's orange! My favorite!' Evidently Cynthia was wearing orange flavored lip gloss. Orange is Greg's favorite flavor and Tasha knows this. "You are really delicious." Greg whispered quietly. Cynthia laughed as she pushed Greg so that he sat down on the bed. She kneeled before him humbly as a servant girl kneels before her Great King. Cynthia maintained eye contact with Greg the whole time. She reached for his shaft maintaining continued eye contact. Her hands were warm and gentle as she stroked him and made him even harder; even longer. She leaned in and took him into her mouth, slowly, and deliberately. "Oh my, my, my." Greg exhaled as he was becoming addicted to the provocative sound of her sucking on his penis, "It's been a minute since I had a blow job girl. I almost forgot how good . . ." He tapered off due to pleasure overload. For Cynthia, this was a good sign. She felt like she was getting through to him. She continued patiently stimulating her man while mentally preparing for the next move. Greg couldn't tell this was a plan. Hell, at this point, he didn't care anymore. He just wanted to please Cynthia; that's all. Cynthia moved Greg to the center of the bed laying him on his back. She straddled him positioning his manhood to slide right inside of her. The light from the candles in the bedroom flickered. Both of the lovers were primed and ready to start the intimate dance. At this precise moment Cynthia paused. She didn't move. She just stared deep into Greg's eyes. Greg was a little confused. He didn't know why she stopped. She had his undivided attention. She then spoke in a whisper so that only Greg could hear her. "Greg, I want to make a deal with you." Then she paused again for emphasis. "Yes. Of course, what is it?" Greg questioned curiously. "It's just between you and I." Cynthia paused again. She leaned forward and worked her hips just a little bit. She didn't want him to lose his erection. "Are you teasing me?" Greg asked. "No, I just want you to agree to the terms of the deal." Cynthia said being purposely mysterious. "Ok, what are the terms of the deal?" Greg requested. She didn't respond with words. She started working her hips again, riding on top of him, and grinding forcefully. This time with more intensity, and being more deliberate. Then she stopped. "No babe, this is not how this deal works," She explained, "we are having sex now. Really great sex. I need you to show me that you trust me. Greg, show me that you trust me completely. I want you to agree to the terms of the deal before you hear the deal."

"Hmmmm, I get it," Greg replied thinking deeply, "is this contingent on me getting sex tonight?" "No. Not at all. Tonight, and every night, I will serve you. I will please you," Cynthia promised, "it's not that kind of deal." Then she really starting ramping it up, winding her hips even faster. As his pleasure almost became unbearable. "Oh my, uhhh, ohhh, you're gonna make me explode girl." Greg sighed. "You like that, don't you?" She proudly stated. "Hmmm, yeah that was great," he admitted. "Back to our deal, are you willing to fully and faithfully commit to my deal without knowing the terms? In other words, do you trust Cynthia Heart, with your whole heart?" "Hmmm, do I get time to think about it?" Greg asked. "Look, either you trust me or you don't," she commented, "no amount of time is going to change that." Cynthia leaned forward resting her weight on her hands with her face inches from Greg's face. Her tender breasts dangling before him. She started working it again. This time gentler. This time a lot slower. She smiled at him and reminded him, "There is a such thing as slow pussy too." They both laughed. "Ok, ok . . ." Greg muttered slowly like he was convincing himself to do it, "I accept your terms without hearing them. I promise to keep my side of the deal faithfully and loyally. Cynthia Heart, you have my word." "And I am your heart." she playfully added. "And you are my heart." Greg replied obediently. "And I am Delicious" She announced deliberately. "And you are very Delicious." He repeated. "And you will never hurt me." She continued. "And Cynthia Heart, I will never hurt you," He recited, "so, what is this deal?" She began to work that thing around and around in circles.

It was like she was celebrating. She didn't answer for a few minutes. All the while driving Greg crazy with her sexual pleasuring techniques. "I think you are showing off," Greg told her, "you know that you are driving crazy." "I know," Cynthia replied, "Greg, sometimes it's good to be bad." "Maybe" he speculated. "Ok, here's the deal," she said, "are you ready? Here is what you signed your name to without knowing the consequences. Are you nervous?" "No, not at all," he replied confidently, "you are trying to make me nervous. I can read you girl." "Really?" she asked. "Really." He responded. "Ok Greg, I need you to help me . . .," she paused to think of something crazy to say, "Rob a bank!" "Ahhh, I knew you were trying to make me nervous," Greg told her, "Now you are a comedian. A delicious sexy comedian at that." "Orange flavored comedian baby!" Cynthia laughed, "Ok, I'm being serious now. It's about our threesome of course. You are a vital part of this thing and I am not going to put more pressure on you, but if you make love to me tonight with all your heart, mind, and power, then I promise I will follow you, listen to you, and obey you. Greg, I will give you my undying loyalty, you will be my Prince, my King, and my Master. It's as simple as that. I want you to give it to me tonight like you never loved any woman before me. Greg, I need you to let go. It's time for you to let go. Tonight baby, you have to give me your all, it has to be personal, real and passionate. No substitutes - no artificial flavors - no fear. You have to give Cynthia Heart your whole heart for one night." "Wow girl. You blew me away with that. I didn't see that one coming." Greg explained. Being genuinely surprised, Greg knew how serious a commitment that Cynthia was talking about. He was shocked that she would go that far. Greg thought to himself for a moment, Cynthia was kinda getting a little nervous herself because Greg was silent in thought. 'Would he follow through or would he fold?' She thought to herself. 'Did I put too much on him? Can he handle it?' Her fear was rising. She was beginning to doubt and worry when she felt his hands touch her face. Holding her face gently in his hands he told her, "Your Prince needs to get to work." The biggest smile came across Cynthia's face that Greg had ever seen. She was glowing like a glistening shining white angel at the top of a Christmas tree. It was on!

Greg rolled his delicious dessert over on her back and he announce loudly, "Let the games begin!" Cynthia laughed out loud. She was on cloud nine having a good time. Greg spread her legs and leaned on them as he began to thrust himself inside of her repeatedly. She was rocking to the rhythm of his warm and forceful penetration. With each stroke she said, "Uh!" at a high pitch. Greg thought to himself, 'She's a screamer.' He never noticed that before. Screamers let you know what the score is. They let you know how you are doing. That's reassuring to men trying to please a woman. Within this moment, Greg completely forgot about Tasha. That was Cynthia's plan from the beginning which she explained to Tasha in detail ahead of time. Greg was busy performing his challenge. He was determined to keep his end of the bargain. He was going to make passionate love to this delicious woman. Greg was a man possessed. He masterfully made love to this beautiful stranger. Cynthia was not prepared for the hurricane named Greg. She started the engine, but she had no idea how fast and how far this sports car was going to go. She was melting under his fiery passion. On this night Cynthia Heart was starting to fall in love. Greg whispered to her, "Lean back, roll over. No, no, no this way. That's it, that's' it. Keep it right there." He uttered these commands like a brilliant general directing an army during a fierce battle, yet he was compassionately caring for her well-being and concerned about her pleasure. "Oh yeah. Oh my God you are sooooo sexy." Cynthia loved the comment "You are sooooo sexy." That simple compliment made her feel good deep inside and made her relax completely. Cynthia craves verbal affirmation because she never received any as a child. As a child growing up in a military household, she was taught to be tough and don't worry what others think or say about you. Greg could sense this. Finally, he was getting through to this delicious angelic creature who seemed so far away from him previously. His confidence was growing with each rhythmic thrust. With each penetration, he was becoming the man, her man, and her king. Delicious was a fitting nickname for Cynthia once you passed her slightly cynical outer shell; a sensuously sweet girl awaited you.

Cynthia protected herself by being guarded and didn't let men get too close to her, but this Friday evening, a compassionate young man was breaking down that wall methodically brick by brick. Something was changing in this bedroom. The intimacy was growing ever stronger with each passing moment. Greg was getting to her. She was melting. She was finally letting go for the first time since Travis Bryant her first true love. Greg didn't know anything about Cynthia's first true love Travis. Hell, Greg couldn't care less about Travis, yet Greg was Travis reincarnated. Cynthia was falling in true love and this wasn't in her plans. She was just trying to get Greg to be comfortable having sex with her so they could continue the threesome. Tasha was still at the door listening. All the thrusting, panting, and moaning in pleasure, indicated that Cynthia had accomplished her mission. Tasha was glad because it meant they could continue the threesome and have more fun with exploration. Tasha didn't realize what was going on in Cynthia's heart. The student had become the master in the bedroom that fateful Friday night. Cynthia, with all of her pyscho-babble, was becoming a young college girl who had found real love for the first time. Greg was becoming a powerful man. A powerful man who had control of two sexy, beautiful, and intelligent women. What could go wrong?

After our two love birds were taking a breather, guess who popped back into the room? "Hmmm, somebody had some fun tonight," Tasha said, "did she wear you out, babe?" "Ahhh, yeah, I guess you could say it like that." Greg replied a little winded. Cynthia felt so guilty. It's like she had betrayed her friend. Every time Tasha looked at her, she felt like Tasha could see into her soul. So, she was very apologetic. "Tasha, I'm so sorry. We completely lost track of time," Cynthia explained, "He was going and I was..., well, I know it's your turn now so I will get out of here for you. You know, I keep forgetting that we are doing this in your bed. Next time you guys are coming over to my place. I have plenty of room." "Relax girl," Tasha reassured her, "All that matters is that our friend Greg had a good time tonight. He finally let loose. That is good, but it's like they say, 'I love it when a plan comes together.'" She walked around the bed to get a high five from Cynthia. Cynthia couldn't help but feel guilty, and Greg noticed it, but Tasha didn't. Cynthia gathered her things so fast and was gone in a flash. Greg was thinking, "What just happened? What did I do to Cynthia? Is she feeling guilty because she is breaking the rules? Is she actually falling in love with me? Is our deal still on?

Chapter Four
| Paradise |

"Hey, how are you?" Greg asked. "I'm great." Cynthia replied. "You ok?" Greg asked, "You left out pretty fast last night. I need to know that you are ok, and that everything is ok. You scared me by leaving so fast." "Yeah, I'm fine," Cynthia said, "everything is good." "Hello, hello. I may have the wrong number here," Greg joked, "I'm trying to speak to Mrs. Delicious. The sexy hot girl I had in the bed last night. She took off so fast that she didn't give me a kiss, or say goodbye or anything. Ya know, she didn't even say she enjoyed the sex and I really tried hard to please her. I don't know if she even enjoyed it. Hell, I don't know if she even remembered it. We made a deal. A deal of a lifetime. I want to know if it is still on. You got to give me something here Cynthia Heart. Talk to me now and tell me the whole truth; no secrets - nothing artificial." "Hmmm ok," Cynthia started to explain, "I owe you the truth, but it's hard to say. First of all, last night was magic. You did so well. It's not the multiple positions, nor the actual sex, which was very, very good by the way. It was your honesty and your real passion I felt. When we were making love, something happened to me. Baby, something deep inside started to come alive. It took me over. I was captivated by it. It was overpowering. Only you Greg could bring it out in me. As for why I left so abruptly, I can't tell you that on the phone. Why don't you meet me in an hour at the fancy restaurant we went to after shopping for Tasha's birthday gifts." "Ok," Greg replied, "I will meet you there on one condition." "What's that?" She asked. "That you wear that short, sexy white party dress you had on the first time we went there." Greg suggested. "As you wish my King," She responded submissively, "I hope the staff there doesn't think I only have one dress." They both laughed. Once they arrived at the restaurant, they greeted each other with a big hug and a passionate kiss. While seated at the restaurant their conversation began with a question. "You know what you're getting?" Greg asked. "Yeah, I'll probably get the same thing I had last time," Cynthia shared. "You wanted to tell me something in person," Greg asked, "why couldn't you tell me over the phone?" "I didn't want Tasha to over hear it." Cynthia confessed. "Well, what's the deal?" Greg questioned. "Look Greg, I feel guilty," Cynthia admitted, "Tasha trusted me and I'm falling in love with her man. This was not what we planned. Every time she looks at me I feel sick to my stomach." "Well, I knew something was wrong," Greg disclosed, "Tasha suspects nothing. So just go with the flow until you start falling out of love." "Hey, I'm not the only one falling in love here am I?" Cynthia requested sternly as she stared him in his face. "Yes, there is something going on here between us," Greg acknowledged, "I lost myself last night. I completely forgot about Tasha until she came back in the room at the end. I felt a little guilt, but I let it go. Remember this was Tasha's idea." "Yes, I know that." She expressed. "Well, the only thing we can do is either end this threesome, or grin & bear it." Greg explained trying to be honest. "Hey, we haven't even got to the fun stuff yet," Cynthia identified a little disappointed, "last night was the second time meeting together as a threesome. We may as well keep going and enjoy the time we have together." "You are probably right," Greg agreed, "I don't have a better idea at this point." They enjoyed their meals and left the restaurant.

Later during the week Cynthia called Tasha. "Hey lady," Cynthia greeted, "how are you?" "Great, great," Tasha replied, "Greg did really well last week, right?" "Oh my goodness," Cynthia confirmed, "girl, I lost track of the time and I felt so bad. But let me tell you he did great. He really let go." "Tell me about it," Tasha demanded, "what did he do to you? I heard you moaning, and there were a couple of subdued, but high-pitched screams too girl." "Really, you heard all that?" Cynthia asked. "Ok, since we don't have any secrets, the truth is," Tasha confessed, "I was sitting by the door listening. I couldn't hear everything, but I know the sound of intense sexual pleasure when I hear it." "Oh my Tasha," Cynthia replied a little scared, "Did you hear my proposal to Greg?" "No, you were so close to him when you said it, I couldn't hear it." Tasha shared. "I asked him to make love to me with all his might." Cynthia told Tasha, "Evidently that worked." "Look, you must have said something else to him," Tasha inquired, "because he was highly motivated. I heard him flipping you over and over like pancakes on Sunday morning girl. I've never seen him so motivated. What is the secret? I want to get some of that from him too." "Well, can I give you some advice?" Cynthia asked. "Yes, lay it on me," Tasha replied, "I'm all ears and open to suggestions." "I started off with a blowjob." Cynthia revealed. "He really liked that. I'm guessing he doesn't get that very often. Right? Look, this is none of my business." "Yeah, you're right, not so much," Tasha admitted, "he's always going down on me and that really gets me going. Then before I know it, he's making love to me slowly." "Yes, I understand," Cynthia responded in a gentle way, "but here's the deal; this must go two ways. He takes care of your needs then you should reciprocate and take care of his needs. I think the blowjob got his attention, then I got on top of him. This is a very important position Tasha. This position gives the woman complete control. It gives the woman power because you are running things. You can reverse it if your man likes to see your booty. If he likes to see your beautiful breasts just face him. But, in the case of Greg, you might need to do both positions. Straddling a man is a real good time to make your requests known to him. I'm just saying." "Preach girl," Tasha said jokingly, "I'm learning so much about him just in the first two Fridays we have done this. So, what's next?" "Ok," Cynthia detailed, "first of all, if it's ok with you guys, we are adding my house as a location for the Friday night rendezvous. We will go there this Friday. You are going to love my home. I call it Paradise. I have everything there for you. It's gonna be so good I promise. We may end up doing it at my house all the time. This is to be determined in the future. Let's take this guy to a strip club so we can see what kind of women he likes. I prefer the upscale clubs. They are classier and we can find all kind of girls there. What do you think? If we find a girl he likes, I'm gonna bring her home for his private entertainment." "What? Are you serious?" Tasha asked in disbelief.

"Look these are high class girls," Cynthia specified, "The girls are clean, they require regular medical checkups of their girls, and we are not catching anything from the girls at this club. Just like we got ourselves checked out before we started this threesome stuff, so too these girls are checked out medically. That's why I prefer this particular classy club to the others. I've already done the research." "But to have a private dance at home is gonna cost thousands I'm sure." Tasha replied concerned. "Don't you worry your pretty little head about that Tasha," Cynthia said with a reassuring tone, "you rollin' with Cynthia Heart aka Big Money Cynt! I got this." They both laughed. "And while Greg is in the back room enjoying the gyrations of some stripper chick," Cynthia continued, "the girls are gonna be in the front room watching some gyrations also; Male Strippers!!! Wooohooo!" "What?! Cynthia, you off the chain girlfriend!" Tasha blurted out genuinely surprised, "I did not know you rolled like that! You know what they say, you got to keep your eye on the quiet ones." "Tasha, it's like I always say," Cynthia told her, "sometimes it's good to be bad." They both fell out laughing. "So, this is how this Friday is going to go down," Cynthia started explaining the plan, "After work we meet at my place, we have a meal, and we can take a shower getting ready to go to the strip club. Say we get to the club around 10pm. Then we will hang out to around midnight or so, hopefully we will find Greg a sexy chick to entertain him. We come back to Paradise (my home) with the stripper girl. Greg and the girl can go to the back room and she can dance for him. The male strippers will arrive at our place at 12:30 a little after midnight.

I will invite several other women from the job to enjoy and tip these well-endowed beasts. I hope you are ready Tasha. I just hope you are ready, for your sake, because you are going to be blown away!" "Oh, I'm ready girl," Tasha stated, "I hope you are ready. I hope you can keep up girlfriend." The girls told Greg the plan for next Friday. "I'm down," Greg declared, "'cause you know I don't want to see some male strippers, I'd much rather see some female strippers."

This time, Friday couldn't come fast enough for all members of the threesome club. They were all excited. Tasha and Greg rode together to Cynthia's house. When they got out of the car, they were floored. "Are you sure this is the correct address?" Tasha asked. "Ummm..., yeah I checked it twice." Greg replied. "Un-fricking believable!" Tasha exclaimed, "This is a modern palatial mansion." "How can Cynthia own this place?" Greg asked in disbelief, "This is a million dollar home or pretty close to it. She doesn't make enough money at her job to pay the taxes on this place; much less the mortgage." "Welcome, welcome, welcome to my humble abode." Cynthia announced as she came out of her home to greet her friends. "You've been holding out on us baby," Greg told her, "your place is magnificent." "I will give you a tour," Cynthia replied laughing, "for free. The first time is free." They walked into this huge house in utter amazement. "Let's go upstairs." Cynthia announced. There were four huge bedrooms upstairs each with a bathroom and a beautiful walk-in shower. From the balcony of one of the bedrooms, you could see the pool, the tennis court, and the basketball court. On the main floor was the master bedroom, another bedroom, and a huge area we will call the living room. There was a gigantic kitchen and a wonderful dining room. Downstairs was a basement like you have never seen. There was a game room, a movie room, a sauna, and a music room. Tasha and Greg were blown away. "How did you keep this place a secret from me? We are best friends." Tasha asked. "I don't let anyone know about my place. So please keep it a secret." Cynthia entreated, "When I invite people over, I tell them my friend is an NFL running back and when he's out of town he lets me use this place. So that is my story, and 'we are sticking to it.' Right friends?" "Right..., right...." Greg uttered slowly. "Let's get some grub." Cynthia pronounced. Rose is the head of Cynthia's in-home staff. She's the one person that Cynthia depends on and trusts completely. She is completely in sync with Cynthia. Often times just a glance from Cynthia indicates a command, and no words need even be spoken between the two to get things done. When they entered the dining area Rose was present. She announced to everyone, "This way to the buffet honored guests." Walking into the kitchen was quite a banquet of exceptional food laid out before them. There was chicken, fish, shrimp, barbeque ribs, and steak for starters. There was also salad, various types of vegetables, croissants, and even a large selection of desserts. It was very similar to a Vegas style buffet. The food was wonderful. "Holy Moses!" Greg exclaimed, "This can't be real Cynthia. How could you afford this?" "Greg I spare no expense for my friends." Cynthia conveyed. The threesome sat in the dining room and ate. Rose brought them their drinks and saw to their every desire. It was mind blowing. After the meal, Greg and Tasha were taken upstairs to their rooms. Tasha and Greg's rooms both had showers. After they showered, both of them had nice attire laid out on their bed for each one of them. Tasha had a very short sexy orange party dress. Tasha knew immediately this was no $60 party dress off Amazon. No, this dress was Saint Laurent and it was worth $2,700 to $3,400 dollars. "Oh my," Tasha practically shouted, "this dress is gorgeous!" There was a stylish suit of similar quality and price laid out for Greg on his bed. There was a pair of slacks, a pullover shirt, and a sports jacket. "Oh yeah," he muttered under his breath, "I can wear this." Cynthia was dressed to kill in a beautiful stunning red party dress of the highest quality. The threesome was going to draw a lot of attention tonight. They would be the best dressed people in the club for sure. Cynthia had Rose call the limo. They walked out to the limo, got in, and headed to the club.

Cynthia made a phone call as we all got settled in the limo. "Yeah, and invite Tonya and Olivia too," Cynthia said smiling, "the fun starts at 12:30 tonight. Don't be late, and don't be scared girl." Call ends. "Cynthia, everything has been so wonderful," Tasha shared, "This is the most expensive dress I've every worn. The food was awesome and your place is spectacular. It's all been mind-blowing." "I'm so glad the two of you are having fun," Cynthia added, "that's why we did this thing to have fun." Tasha and Greg were sitting together in the back of the limo while Cynthia was sitting opposite facing them. Cynthia moves toward Greg and sits on the other side of him. "Greg, you have two beautiful women on your right and on your left," Cynthia stated, "You are truly the man tonight, isn't he Tash?" "Yes he is!" Tasha answered like she was giving the preacher an 'amen' at church. "Since we won't be with you tonight, Tasha and I decided to give you a surprise on the way to the club," Cynthia revealed, "So now you can cross 'a blow job in the back of a limo' off your bucket list." Tasha turned to him and gave him a sexy smile. "Really?" Greg responded as Cynthia started massaging his member slowly. "Yeah really," Cynthia whispered in his ear. She began kissing him on his neck and getting him aroused. "Cynthia, is that mango flavor on your lips?" Greg asked. "You like orange. I like mango," Cynthia answered, "maybe next time I will get orange/mango flavor so we both can be happy." She continued kissing him. Cynthia started to notice a rise from Greg's pants. "Ya know Tasha," Cynthia announced, "sometimes things can get hard." "That's my cue," Tasha replied, "I'm up next baby." Tasha got on her knees in front of her boyfriend and unzipped his pants. "Tasha, have you ever seen a man refuse a perfectly good blow job?" Cynthia questioned, "I really don't think it is possible. It would be a first. A world's record. You can't go wrong with a blow job girl." While Tasha was dutifully handling things down below, Cynthia started kissing her lover passionately. She took her sexy red dress completely off so that Greg could admire her naked breasts that swayed with the rocking of the limo. Cynthia was taking advantage of the fact that Tasha was preoccupied with her mouth stimulating Greg down low. This allowed her some private time with Greg. So she began to kiss Greg and whisper into his ear. "Baby, you know I arranged this for you because I love you. I know you will like it," She whispered, "I'm yours. You can do whatever you want with me. You are my Prince - my King - my Master. Please never forget that. Just ask me to do something, anything, and I will obey. It will be a labor of love. Do you hear me babe?" "Yeah, yeah. I hear you." Greg whispered softly. This double stimulation was sending him into a bit of a trance; just as Cynthia had planned. Cynthia quickly put her dress back on as they arrived at the club. Greg zipped his pants up and got out of the limo with Tasha. After Cynthia exited the limo, she approached the limo driver to tell him something. As they entered the club, they welcomed them inside and each of them replied thanks in their own way. The club was beautiful. The music was not too loud and there were a lot of powerful people here such as judges, politicians, CEO's, business owners, etc. The threesome walked in like they owned the place. Greg had all eyes on him because he had two gorgeous sexy black princesses on his arms. Guys looking at Greg were vocally asking themselves, "How did he pull that off?" This attention was going to Greg's head. In this moment Greg was really the man. Cynthia guided them smoothly through the club like she knew her way around. She led them to an area in the club where there were two runways for the strippers to walk down. One on the left and the other on the right. She seated them right in the middle so they could see both runways. "This is a good place to sit," Cynthia explained, "this way you can see both runways and check out more girls quicker. Because what we are trying to do is find Greg a couple of hot girls to take back to Paradise." "Cool," Greg responded, "I get to decide which girls?" "Of course," Cynthia voiced. "Ok, then how many girls am I looking for?" Greg solicited. "Two is all you can handle," Cynthia answered, "don't try to kill yourself the first night in the club." "Ok," Greg conceded, "two it is."

Tasha went to the bar to get some drinks for everyone. While she was gone Cynthia spoke with Greg. "You can get three girls if you want," She whispered, "I didn't want to say that in front of Tasha. She thinks these girls are just strippers." "What are you saying Cynthia?" Greg asked very curiously. "Are these high-class call girls?" "This is a very elite club," Cynthia explained, "You can get whatever you are willing to pay for. I'm taking care of my man tonight. Different girls have different prices based on their experience, beauty, and popularity. Greg, you choose whichever girls you like and enjoy them. Tasha, me, and the ladies from the office will be in the front room being entertained by the male strippers. Tasha will not know what you are doing in the back. I will keep her occupied for you." "Are these girls ok? Are they clean?" Greg asked. "Yes, they have regular checkups and believe me I wouldn't be here. Don't worry I've taken care of everything. Just enjoy yourself." Cynthia said. Tasha came back with the drinks for everyone. Cynthia told Tasha that she wanted to play a little game with her; a betting game. "Let's see who between us can guess which girls Greg will like." Cynthia challenged, "If you win, I will buy you another Saint Laurent dress or any brand of the same caliber of your choice. If I win, you have to go on vacation with me. I will pay all of the expenses and you have to participate in all the activities I participate in. No exceptions." "Ohhhh, I can get another dress like this," Tasha stated with excitement, "hell yeah!! You're on girlfriend!!" "Let the games begin!" Cynthia announced. "Oh, and by the way, we're going to go with three girls not two." "Why?" Tasha asked being a little concerned. "No worries. I think Greg is a big boy," Cynthia joked, "I think he can handle three strippers. Hell, you only live once." Greg became the hunter as all these scantily clad women came strutting down the runway. He verbalized, "These are truly higher-class girls than in the other clubs. Look at their bodies. Not an ounce of fat in the wrong place, and have you noticed they keep looking at me in the face for some reason. I know you think I'm on an ego trip, but I'm not. They are looking at me trying to get my attention." "Greg," Cynthia started explaining, "what you have to realize is these girls are scoping out the audience to see if they see some influential, rich, or popular guy. Then they focused their attention on that guy to get him aroused. They can't figure you out. They have never seen you before and you are wearing a very expensive suit which they recognize. They think you must be rich; maybe an internet millionaire or a small business man. You could be someone who has flown under the radar. These girls are good at what they do. They will select you and make you think you've selected them. So be careful Greg. Choose wisely."

Right then a sexy girl came prancing down the runway who caught Greg's eye. She was about 5ft 6' wearing a pink teddy. This exquisitely beautiful black girl had it going on. Cynthia immediately wrote her down on a napkin: Black girl in pink teddy - Priscilla. A few more girls strolled by, but no one caught his eye. On the other runway, a Puerto Rican Princess came strolling down. Dark curly hair, full figure, and enchanting light blue eyes. She was wearing a skimpy two-piece dark blue bathing suit. Cynthia wrote her down: Puerto Rican blue bathing suit - Tatiana. Soon after on the other runway, a beautiful white girl came down about 5ft 8', blond with light brown eyes, and wearing a red babydoll outfit. There was something about her. Cynthia could tell she was trying to get Greg's attention. Cynthia took a chance and wrote her down too: white girl in red babydoll get up - Angel.

Those were her three choices. She felt good about them and was sure she would win the contest between her and Tasha. "Hey, it's getting close to the time for us to leave," Cynthia acknowledged, "What are your choices Greg? Have you found your entertainment for the evening?" "Yes, yes, and yes," Greg replied playfully, "There are three, count them, three charming ladies that caught my eye. Drum roll please. . . . Priscilla, Tatiana, and Angel." "Ok here are my picks." Tasha said while handing her napkin to Cynthia. "Let's see who you picked. . . Ok, you got Priscilla, but you didn't pick Tatiana, or Angel." Cynthia pointed out, "Here is my paper: Priscilla, Tatiana, and Angel! I win, I win," Cynthia shouted excitedly, "we're going on vacation! We're going on vacation! Don't worry Tasha, we both win because I'm taking you shopping for that very expensive dress anyway." "Wooohooo!" Tasha exclaimed. She was jazzed. That night everyone was a winner at the strip club. Cynthia, Tasha, and of course, Greg. "So how did you know?" Tasha asked. "I simply paid attention to Greg's response to each girl coming down the runway." Cynthia shared, "Although he looked at each girl carefully, I could tell when he was giving special attention to a girl. Plus consider what's his type. He likes you Tasha. You are built just like Priscilla, and Tatiana falls into your category as well. Angel was a longshot. I didn't know if Greg liked white girls or not. But Angel is my height and has a similar build as I do. Plus the light brown eyes would remind him of you Tasha. If he likes a white girl, this would be the one that he likes. It was an educated guess." "Hmmm…, interesting." Tasha answered.

Cynthia went and spoke with the manager of the club to arrange an offsite party with Priscilla, Tatiana, and Angel. They were all available and willing to do the gig. Greg would have them for 3 hours. "How much?" Tasha asked, she had to know. "Hmmm, three thousand dollars a girl," Cynthia replied, "and an extra five hundred dollars per girl for the last-minute notice." "Ten thousand five hundred dollars for 3 hours," Tasha said, "that sounds like the price of a high-classed call girl." "Inflation is real girl." Cynthia reminded her. They all jumped into the limo and headed back to Paradise. Once they got back to Paradise, Cynthia's place, they got Greg set up in a spacious bedroom with a large bathroom. In the interim, the ladies from Tasha's job started arriving. The maid took them to the living room and offered them a bite to eat. The girls from the club arrived first right on time. They brought their own music for the show and set up in the same spacious bedroom to entertain Greg. The male strippers arrived soon thereafter and the party in the living room area began. From Greg's location, he could faintly hear an occasional, "Whew!! Take it off, take it off!" from the girls having too much fun in the living room. Nonetheless, Greg soon realized the stripper girls were not here to simply take off their clothes. They each stripped one at a time starting with the Puerto Rican girl Tatiana. "Wow." Greg was very aroused. Then the gorgeous black girl did her thing. Greg was beyond aroused. Finally, Angel started to reveal her young naked body to Greg with a lot of gyration, bouncing titties, and booty shaking. One by one they approached Greg sitting there on the bed, and little by little, his clothes started mysteriously coming off. Greg already had two girls. Now he was expected to have sex with three girls. Greg just hoped that Tasha didn't drop in on this scene.

Meanwhile, in the living room, there were four male strippers who were earning their money. These ladies were going crazy. It's like they never saw a man before. Along with Tasha and Cynthia, Tonya, Olivia, Jessica, and Tina were also present. Janet was running late, and arrived around 12:45. In all there were seven women from the same job and four male strippers. These guys were buffed and toned with no flab on their fit bodies. "Jessica, have another drink." Cynthia shouted over the music, "Here!" She yelled as she handed her an opened wine cooler." "Does anyone need a drink?" Tasha asked, "We got wine coolers, wine, beer, soda, and sangria. Rose offered to make anyone who wants a daiquiri or any frozen drink." There were a couple of takers. Tasha ran to the kitchen with the orders. Moments later Cynthia came flying into the kitchen to get Tasha. "Girl, you better get your behind out here," Cynthia blurted out with excitement, "they are going to whip it out! Come on!!" The two girls flew out of the kitchen laughing all the way.

Greg literally had his hands full trying to please 3 women at the same time. "Let me show you a trick," Angel suggested, "you are gonna like this Greg." She got on her knees and put a condom on the tip of his dick. She used her lips to unroll the condom down his hard shaft. When she finished his prick was rock solid and it was completely inside her warm mouth. She began to pleasure him slowly. "Look ma, no hands," Priscilla said laughing, "girl you got mad skills." Inside of his mind Greg was getting worried, he knew he couldn't have sex with three gorgeous young women. Maybe he could handle one or two of them, but certainly not all three. Therefore, he started talking to the girls. "So, what do you girls do with your money?" Greg asked, "Do you invest it in the market or in real estate?" No one has ever taken a personal interest in these girls. They didn't even know how to answer the question. "I spend my extra money on the best clothes and shoes I can find." Tatiana admitted. "Me, I take care of my kid and my mom," Priscilla confessed, "and I also save my money." "Hmmm..., I love to take trips," Angel replied, "I'm saving up to go to the islands next month."

"That's all very good," Greg said, "I think you should enjoy some of your money, but the key is to make some of your hard-earned money work for you. You start with a percentage of your money 10%, 15%, or 20%, then you set that aside for investments. You could put it in the market, into real estate, or even start a small business." "Yeah Greg," Priscilla responded, "that makes sense and I can do that, but I know nothing about investing." "Priscilla, you will learn." Greg promised, "With your money on the line you will read books, go on line, find a broker, a real estate broker, or a stock broker. You will do what you need to do to learn. Your financial future depends on it. Let me tell you some good websites that you can use to help you with this." What is so bizarre about this scene is they are having this conversation while being completely naked.

Meanwhile, the party continues in the front of the house. "Ladies, our strong and very talented stripper guys have asked for our help." Cynthia announced, "They tell me there is something that each of us can do to help them stay hard." The girls went wild. "Yeah!!!" they yelled, "We want them to stay hard!!" "I don't know how to say this," Cynthia replied, "they need us to get topless. I'm there." Cynthia dropped her red dress to the floor. She now only had her panties on. "Who's with me!?" The ladies started taking off their blouses and bras were flying all over the place. "Let those puppies breathe!" Someone shouted. It was a mad house in the front room that night. Pure pandemonium was taking place. Imagine a house full of topless horny women who were all slightly drunk; some were very drunk. Titties were bouncing and jiggling all over the place per the request of the male strippers. It was time for one of the strippers, Kevin, to take a break. He was handsome, muscular, athletic, and a gentleman all at the same time. Jessica and Tina followed Kevin upstairs, with drinks in hand, talking with him while he was on his break. They made their way to the upstairs master bedroom. Both of the women were topless, but Jessica had nothing on but panties. She was wearing a dress previously. Tina had a short skirt on. Once these three got in the bedroom, let's just say Kevin didn't get a break at all. They were all over him. Hands down his briefs, panties fell to the floor, kissing, moaning, and stroking him making him hard as steel. "Kevin, I hope you can handle two at a time." Jessica challenged him breathlessly. "Ma'am," Kevin announced, "I aim to please."

In the backroom downstairs the conversation continued. "No one has ever showed any interest in us personally." Priscilla told Greg, "All these guys want is sex with a beautiful girl. Greg, you really helped us out here with your advice. And I promise you we will start investing this money that we make and grow our wealth, making our money work for us. So, we really want to thank you in a very special way." "Oh, boy," Greg responded with a smile, "here we go." Priscilla rolled Greg to the middle of the bed and mounted him just like Cynthia had done. She started working it vigorously. The other girls were looking on giggling and whispering among themselves. It was Priscilla's show and Greg was at her mercy. Priscilla was quite talented in the bedroom and Greg could hardly keep up with this young gorgeous beauty. Greg started thinking. "Priscilla," Greg said catching his breath, "I want to show you something that will give you even greater pleasure." "Ok," she replied, "you know I'm down for that." "Angel, can we borrow your corset?" Greg asked. "Sure." Angel answered as she went into her bag and pulled it out. "You girls give her a hand," Greg encouraged them, "help her put that on. Make sure that it's really tight. I mean extremely tight." "Uhhh," Priscilla exclaimed, "are you trying to kill me. I can barely breathe." "Priscilla trust me," Greg promised, "you will thank me later." Greg took Priscilla and rolled her on her back. He pulled her to the edge of the bed, and spread her legs wide. He began to penetrate her slowly and deeply. As deep as he could go. She started moaning with pleasure. The corset greatly increased the pleasure a woman feels during sex. "Oh, my goodness," Priscilla moaned in extreme pleasure. "Greg, Greg you were right, it feels soooooo good, don't stop, don't stop Greg." Greg continued to satisfy this young luscious chocolate angel. She never had sex like this. She really likes Greg because he cares for her, but Greg was getting tired. It had really been a long day for him. At that moment the door swung open. The girls all gasped at the same time because it startled them. It was Cynthia wearing nothing but her panties and completely drunk. She was slurring her words. "Baby, are you having a good time?" Cynthia muttered, "Oh, you're doing the black girl. Don't stop. I just came back here to let you know that you got 10 more minutes before they have to leave." The young sexy strippers started to get dress and gathered their things.

Greg pulled himself out of Priscilla and declared, "Saved by the bell." He was exhausted, and if it is possible, this man had too much fun in one night. Greg put on his clothes and went to find Tasha. Tasha was knocked out on the couch topless in her panties. Greg woke her up and put her dress back on. He walked her upstairs to the bedroom where she showered and changed in before they went to the club. He laid her down and they talked for a few minutes to make sure everything was ok. She dozed off mid-sentence. Everyone was gone when Greg headed down stairs. The male strippers had left. The ladies from Tasha's job were all too drunk to drive and were taken home in the limo.

Cynthia was wearing a beautiful silk robe when Greg found her in the kitchen. "You girls had a good time?" he asked. "Yeah, it was an absolutely insane night," Cynthia confessed, "I'm bushed." "You," Greg replied emphatically, "I can barely stand up. Those girls wore me out." "I bet they did," Cynthia taunted him, "those young girls will suck you dry, and I mean that literally." They both chuckled. "This is the first Friday night you did not make love to me since we started this threesome thing." "Well, it has only been 3 weeks," Greg clarified, "but I understand your point. You start to get used to it, right?" "Yeah," she replied, "come hold me until I go to sleep." She led Greg to her room, they got in her bed, and Greg held her in his arms until she dozed off.

Greg went to the kitchen to get a snack before going to bed. Rose was cleaning up. She wanted to make sure Greg had a good time that evening. "Master Greg," Rose addressed, "how was your evening?" "Fine ma'am." He responded. "Would you like some hot chocolate with that?" Rose offered. "Sure," Greg replied, "I love hot chocolate." "You are going to really love the way I make it," Rose stated, "no one takes the time to do things right anymore. They always use the chocolate powder to make it. Come sit at the counter and I will show the proper way to make hot chocolate Master Greg." "You know I like to cook?" Greg informed. "I know," Rose replied, "I'm the only person that she can talk to. She tells me a lot, not everything, but I can fill in the blank parts with my imagination and experience in life." "Really?" Greg said. "I could tell there was a telepathic connection between you and Cynthia the first day I met you." "Master Greg," Rose inquired, "you are quite empathic yourself when it comes to women. You read them well don't you?" "Maybe a little better than the average guy." Greg admitted thoughtfully.

Rose was busy chopping up a couple of dark chocolate bars (one 70% coco the other 60%) while she was talking. As a fellow chef, Greg was taking mental notes. She took the whole milk and heated a cup of it up on the stove. Rose put two cinnamon sticks in the hot milk. She placed a sauce pan on the stove and began to melt the dark chocolate bar shavings. Then she took some heavy whipping cream, added 2 teaspoons of brown sugar, a pinch of salt, and a touch of vanilla mixing it up. She poured the heavy cream mixture into the hot milk whisking it as she added it little by little. Once the chocolate was melted, she incrementally poured the hot milk mixture into the chocolate slowly whisking it in little by little until all the milk was poured in. "Voila!" Rose announced. "Master Greg, that is how you make hot chocolate." "Oh my," Greg responded after tasting it, "it is sooo thick and sooo much chocolate flavor with a hint of cinnamon. Mrs. Rose you are the best!" "So how were the three young ladies you had with you in the back room?" Rose asked. Greg felt a little funny talking to the head of Cynthia's staff about that kind of stuff, so he hesitated a moment trying to figure out what to say. Rose noticed the hesitation and added, "Master Greg, I run this whole house. There is nothing that I don't know that goes on here. If these girls didn't perform their duties fully, I will report them to the Club for disciplinary action. It's my job to make sure our guests are treated appropriately." "Of course," Greg explained, "the girls were fine. They all did a good job. No need to report any of them." "So, you are quite the stud Master Greg," Rose said with a smile, "you conquered 3 young beautiful girls in three hours." "Ok Mrs. Rose," Greg confessed, "this is strictly between you and I. Don't tell Cynthia and my goodness, please don't tell Tasha. I only enjoyed the black girl. We kinda connected a little. The other girls just danced and did their strip routines for me, but that is between you and I Mrs. Rose, right?" "Your secret is safe with me," Rose confirmed, "you seem like a decent man to me. How did you convince these two beautiful girls, Tasha and Cynthia, to do this threesome thing?" "Trust me Mrs. Rose," Greg said forcefully, "It was not my idea! I had nothing to do with it! This is Tasha's and Cynthia's idea. I kinda just got caught up in it. At first it was difficult for me, but as time went on, I loosened up." "These girls today are crazy," Rose told him, "who would take their man, a perfectly good man and give him to your best girlfriend for her to try him own for size? It's a really bad plan." "I know," Greg responded, "you are preaching to the choir. Thanks for the excellent hot chocolate and good night Mrs. Rose." "Good night Master Greg," Rose said appreciative of the conversation, "and good luck with everything." After saying good night, he went upstairs to his room and went straight to sleep.

Chapter Five
|Tasha's Birthday|

Tasha's birthday was coming up and it would be on a Tuesday. Cynthia and Greg had planned a surprise party at Cynthia's residence. Her abode, affectionately called Paradise, was quickly becoming the favorite location of the threesome for obvious reasons. Cynthia was going to invite some people from work. Greg was going to invite some of her old friends such as those friends she grew up with and some from high school. The way the surprise would work, Cynthia will invite Tasha over to go shopping for the expensive dress she promised Tasha at the club. When Tasha comes over to go shopping, everyone would be there and they would jump out and scream, "SURPRISE!" And as for the shopping date to buy this expensive dress, Cynthia would have several of these prominent clothing stores send someone over with a selection of dresses in Tasha's size coupled with Cynthia's taste. Saint Laurent and the other clothing elites set up several racks of clothes on the patio next to the pool. These girls were going shopping right there at Cynthia's home. This was just one part of a wonderful birthday which Greg and Cynthia planned for Tasha. Greg took Tuesday off. While Tasha was at work, Greg had a brand-new washer installed at her place. He made a video of the whole process showing the guys removing the old washer and putting in the brand-new modern washing machine Tasha wanted. He also went and got her some spectacular flowers; lots of them.

He also picked up a large box of Godiva chocolates; Tasha's favorite. The last two gifts, the diamond necklace and a set of large high quality white towels, he would give her at her birthday party in person after showing everyone the video of the washer being installed. The staff at Paradise laid out a birthday banquet of food like no other. There was filet mignon, ribs, oxtails, lobster, shrimp, fish, chicken, and any other thing your heart could desire. Moreover, don't leave out the desserts. There was ice cream (Haagen-Dazs, Ben & Jerry's, Blue Bell, Baskin Robins), cakes, pies, and cookies. The drinks that were available were vintage wines and beers. There were freshly squeezed juices (like pomegranate and orange juice blend, pineapple and mango and orange juice with a hint of coconut), they had mixed drinks, and frozen alcoholic beverages of all kinds. Cynthia spared no expense for her best friend. Family and friends were deeply impressed. They were blown away wondering, who could afford to throw such a party like this? Everything went off without a hitch.

When Tasha showed up, she was invited into the huge living room by Rose. Cynthia comes out and hugs Tasha. "Are you ready to go shopping girl?" Cynthia asked, "Wait a moment. I can't find my keys. Could you look in the kitchen for me? I will check my bedroom." Tasha makes her way to the kitchen and as she turns the corner, "Surprise!!!!!" Tasha's reaction was priceless, authentic just like her love for Greg. Her smile and how she looked around at the people she knew loved her said it all. Tears of I missed you, I can't believe you're here, and I love you so much were released by

Tasha. Everyone began approaching Tasha to hug her. The atmosphere was filled with words saying, "I haven't seen you since forever." "Where have you been hiding?" "You need to come and visit your aunt sometime. I ain't getting no younger." "Where did you find this guy girl? He is so fine." "This is quite a spread, who could afford this?" "Hey, can you hook a brother up with Cynthia? Damn she fine."

Greg announced, "It's time for me to give my birthday gift to my Angel who grows younger and more beautiful every day." "Ahhhh," a chorus of women said. "I just wanna know when's the wedding!" Someone shouted from the kitchen. Everyone laughed. On the wall of the living room, Greg had the video he recorded play so everyone could see. It was the video of the men installing her new washing machine. Tasha gave Greg a big hug and kiss. She thanked him being completely surprised a second time. "But that's not all," Greg said as he pulled a huge bag from behind the couch, "these are white hypoallergenic towels to replace the colored towels you have in your house. My baby's skin is irritated by those dyes in the colored towels." At that moment it all came together in Tasha's mind. These gifts are a result of going shopping with Cynthia. "Where is Cynthia?" Tasha asked looking around, "Girl, I know how he knows exactly what I want!" Cynthia yelled back to Tasha from across the room, "I'm just a secret agent doing her job." "Now for the 'pièce de résistance'." Greg told everyone. "What is that? What does it mean?" a voice questioned from the back. "It's French. It means the main dish, the main thing." Greg explained as he pulled out a long thin box. He opened it and presented it to Tasha. She got weak and began to tear up. "I don't believe it." She said as he put this gorgeous necklace around her neck. Are those real diamonds?" Someone questioned looking on? "Ahhhhhhh," was heard at a low volume throughout the crowd. "Girl you know you can't wear that in the hood!" Someone blurted out obnoxiously. "It's just what I wanted!" Tasha exclaimed as she wrapped her arms around Greg giving him a very slow intimate kiss in front of everyone. "Y'all need to get a room. There are kids in here." Someone joked causing everyone to laugh. A few minutes later after the excitement of Greg's gifts settled down, Cynthia came to the front and told the crowd, "Now it's my turn. Hello everyone and welcome to Tasha's birthday party." Cynthia announced, "My name is Cynthia and I've worked with her for some time now. During this time we have become the closest of friends. I find her to be an honest, kind, and brilliant person. Therefore, I wanted to make this birthday her best one yet. I am presenting my presents to her now. Out by the pool are several racks of clothes all in Tasha's size. Only the finest for Tasha. Tasha is to choose at least 3 clothing items from these racks. More if she wants. A long evening gown, a short party dress, and any other dresses that catches her eye." Tasha hasn't looked out by the pool yet. She didn't know what was going on outside.

Tasha went outside by the pool and started shopping. Cynthia joined her. Tasha ended up with 5 unbelievable dresses. Each one was breathtaking. Members of her family were impressed with the wealth and generosity of Tasha's new friend Cynthia. After the shopping extravaganza, everyone trickled back inside. Cynthia then made another announcement. "I'm not finished," Cynthia declared, "I have another gift for Tasha. Come up here Tasha." Tasha made her way through the crowd to Cynthia. Cynthia handed her an envelope. Tasha took it and opened it. There was 100 one-hundred-dollar bills in the envelope. Ten thousand dollars cash!!! "Oh, my God," Tasha expressed with gratitude, "Are you serious? I can't believe it. Thank you Cynt. This is my best birthday ever!" Tasha's friends and family stood there in utter disbelief. They whispered among themselves. "You got to hook me up with Cynthia, Tasha!" Tasha's young cousin yelled from the back. Everyone laughed. "One last thing," Cynthia told everyone, "Tasha and I are going on vacation together. A girl's only trip all-expense paid vacation to Las Vegas. We will be staying at The Venetian Hotel. Here everyone, take a look at it." Using the same device Greg used earlier, Cynthia had beautiful pictures and video of the impressive Venetian Hotel in Vegas displayed in the living room. The 'ooohs' and 'aaahs' just kept rolling naturally from the attendees with each spectacular scene. Once again the friends and family were blown away, Tasha was speechless, but Greg was not happy. You could see the anger on his face. This was not a competition. Greg already told Cynthia in private that he was going to take Tasha to Vegas. He even told her he wanted to take her to The Venetian Hotel. Cynthia not only upstaged Greg; that's fine, she is a millionaire. Still, she stole the idea which now stops Greg from going to Vegas with Tasha. He felt that she knew what she was doing. She was blocking him from connecting and spending time with Tasha alone in Vegas. Cynthia wanted Greg for herself and didn't want Greg spending quality time with Tasha on a trip to Vegas away from her. While the video of The Venetian Hotel was playing, Cynthia was searching around the room to see how Greg was reacting, but she didn't see him. Intuitively she knew a storm was coming. A category five hurricane by the name of Greg. Rose saw Greg avoid Cynthia's gaze by ducking into the kitchen while the video of The Venetian was playing. She knew something was up, but couldn't tell exactly what.

There was a live DJ at the party and she started playing music. The people had a great time. They danced, ate well, talked about this incredible house, and this incredible person named Cynthia. Greg deliberately avoided running into Cynthia. In fact, he left the party for several hours. Rose saw him leave. He called Tasha and asked her when she wanted him to come get her to take her home. "Babe, where are you?" Tasha yelled into her phone over the loud music. "I'm coming back to the party to get you." Greg said. "I don't know babe," Tasha explained, "I think I'm going to stay here overnight. I want to get another orange daquiri." That was not the answer he wanted to hear. Greg wanted to take Tasha to her home and come back to talk to Cynthia alone. He didn't want Tasha to know about this disagreement between Cynthia and himself. "Ok, ok," Greg told her, "no problem. Enjoy yourself. It's your birthday." "Yeah," Tasha responded, "but hurry up and come back. I want to be with you tonight. I want to celebrate my birthday with you." "Ok," Greg replied, "I'm on my way back to you now." He hung out for another hour or so, and returned to Paradise around 10pm. The friends and family had to get home for they all had to work the next day. Everyone started trailing out little by little. "There you are," Tasha said slurring her words. She had one too many Orange Daquiris, "baby I missed you. Did you see the gifts that Cynthia gave me? We are going to Vegas together." "Yeah, that's great babe," Greg replied mechanically, "I'm happy for you." "And I don't have to spend my ten thousand dollars to go," Tasha continued, "it is an all-expense paid vacation. You can't beat that." "No baby, I can't beat that." Greg told her unenthusiastically. Rose heard the entire conversation from the kitchen. Cynthia was outside saying good bye to her guests. Greg said, "I'm headed upstairs." "I will be up in a minute babe." Tasha slurred out. She wanted to get just one more Daquiri.

Cynthia returned asking, "Where's Greg?" "He's upstairs," Tasha answered, "I'm headed upstairs now. You all have a good night and Cynthia, thank you for your wonderful gifts. This was the best birthday I ever had. Also, thank you Mrs. Rose for your preparation and hard work to accommodate everyone. You did a world class job and I am forever indebted to you. Good night friends." Once upstairs, Greg rubbed the birthday girl down with coconut oil. He gave her a birthday massage. He pampered her and finally, he made sincere passionate love to his girlfriend on her birthday. Tasha was thoroughly pleased about how everything turned out on her birthday. She passed out completely happy and was entirely satisfied.

Greg was steaming! He had a harder time falling to sleep. After breakfast the next morning, Greg was ready to load up the car with all of Tasha's presents to take Tasha home. Cynthia overslept and was just dragging herself out of the bed as Greg and Tasha were loading the car. All three of them had taken the day off in anticipation of a long night on Tasha's birthday. "Why are you guys leaving?" Cynthia asked, "You can hang out if you want. We got the day off." Rose was helping them load the car with the presents. "Well, I'm going to check out my new washer," Tasha answered, "and I want to clear out all my old towels and put the new improved ones up. Besides girl, I got to put this ten thousand in the safe. I can't be walking around with all this cheddar on me. Hotlanta is a dangerous place." They laughed. "Ok," Cynthia said, "happy birthday. You know I love you and if you want to do something later call me. Good bye Greg." Rose waited for his response. "Bye." Greg replied dryly. They drove off.

Greg helped her unload her gifts and he showed her how her new washer worked. After he hugged her, and wishing her a happy birthday again, he left. Greg headed straight back to Paradise. Rose opened the door, "Back so soon?" "Mrs. Rose," Greg announced sternly, "may I please speak with Cynthia?" Rose was thinking in her head, 'You could have spoken with her before you left.' Yet she diplomatically stated, "Absolutely Master Greg." Rose notified Cynthia on the intercom system, "Cynthia, Master Greg is here to speak to you." Then Rose disappeared. Cynthia came around the corner wearing a sexy red lingerie. "Hey Greg," she said innocently, "how are you?" "You prance in here like nothing happened" Greg responded upset. "Baby what's wrong?" Cynthia asked humbly. "Cynthia Heart," Greg stated emphatically, "you know exactly what is wrong. Don't play dumb with me. I can read you." "Ok," Cynthia explained, "So I'm taking the girl with me to Vegas." "No, you are taking her to the very same hotel that I was going to take her to." Greg explained. "You sabotaged my plan. You sabotaged my trip with her to Vegas. I told you about that because I trusted you." "Ok Greg," she tried to appease him as she turned to walk to the living room, "let's just calm down and discuss this like rational adults." "Cynt get your robe." Greg told her. "Oh my goodness," Cynthia replied, "you've seen my naked behind before and liked it a lot, what's the problem now?" "I can't have a serious conversation with you half naked." Greg replied. "I don't want to have a serious conversation with you baby," she told him, "I just want to spend some time with you and I don't want you to be mad at me." "You are so spoiled," Greg responded, "you lack discipline and structure in your life. You get whatever you want - how you want it - when you want it." "And that's wrong?" Cynthia asked, "I earned every penny of the wealth that I possess. I can do with it what I please, and that is not wrong." "Just because you have the power to do something doesn't mean it is right to do it." Greg fired back. "Hmmmm..., ok. I get it." Cynthia replied, "the guy who's fucking his girlfriend's best friend is lecturing me on what is right and wrong." "Oh you got to be kidding me Cynthia," Greg was frustrated beyond measure, "you are trying to play both sides of the fence here. First, you want to be with me. Then when being with me is a problem, you use it against me in an argument. Yes, it is wrong for me to cheat on my girlfriend, but I'm cheating with you! And you are participating voluntarily!" "Ok, ok," Cynthia noted, "there is enough hypocrisy to go around for everyone, I get it. Plus, you are sooooo mad right now. Let me calm you down. Let me satisfy you." "I'm not in the mood to calm down," Greg replied, "have you ever been that mad? I have just been betrayed by someone that I thought I could trust." "Ok, you can trust me baby," Cynthia pleaded with him, "just give me another chance and I will show you I'm for you." "Oh please." Greg said as he sat down. His leg was just going up and down rapidly like he had a nervous twitch. He put his head in his hands and he decided he should leave. He was not getting anywhere trying to reason with this crazy woman. It's like she couldn't see what she did wrong. After a minute or two, Greg got up and headed for the door. "No, no, no, no, don't go," Cynthia said clinging to him, "I apologize, I was wrong. I should have spoken to you about the trip to Vegas ahead of time. I knew you would be mad. I knew it." "Then why Cynt, did you do it?" Greg asked confused. "Because I love you. I want to be with you." Cynthia confessed, "I couldn't help myself. I wasn't going to let her go on a trip with you without me..., now that's the truth Greg, Do you recognize it? It's the same thing I told you at the restaurant. I want to be with you and I get what I want..., most of the time."

Greg was silent for a moment. She was telling the truth finally, and she realized she was wrong. However, the jury is still out on if he could trust her going forward. Rose was around the corner in the kitchen just out of sight. She heard everything and was piecing this puzzle together like a pro. His anger abated a little, but he was still agitated. She took his hand and led him back to the couch in the living room. They sat down and she told him, "Just hold me," and he put his arms around her. No one said a word. Rose walked through the living room. Greg noticed Cynthia sending her a signal. Cynthia just nodded her head towards Rose, and Rose nodded back. These two had some kind of telepathy going on between them. What could that signal mean?

Greg dozed off holding Cynthia. Cynthia started moving in his arms and this woke Greg up. She turned to him as if to wake him up. "What?" Greg asked "I got something for you baby." Cynthia whispered sweetly. "Something for me?" Greg asked, but he didn't understand. "Get up, babe," She told him, "go to the door." "The door?" Greg said confused, "Who is it?" "It's for you Greg." Cynthia was smiling. So Greg went to the door half-way thinking maybe it's Tasha at the door. He opened the door and he was genuinely surprised. It was the most beautiful, young, sexy, and voluptuous black girl he had seen in less than a week. "Priscilla?" Greg asked surprised, "What ah? . . ." Priscilla was smiling from ear to ear. She was really glad to see Greg. Priscilla reached one hand out to him and instinctively he grabbed it. She started walking to the back bedroom pulling him along saying, "We got to finish something that we started the other night." Greg wasn't mad at Priscilla. In fact, he was pleased to see her. Like seeing a long-lost friend that you can really connect with. "Greg, enjoy yourself." Cynthia told Greg as he and his tantalizing companion disappeared down the hallway. Cynthia thought to herself, 'Sometimes it's good to be bad.' She smiled deeply knowing she was making some progress breaking down Greg's barrier little by little. Once in the room, Priscilla started helping Greg take off his clothes. Greg was trying to figure out how Priscilla knew he was there at Paradise and why she would show up? But Priscilla was not answering any questions. Once his clothes were off, she pushed him down causing him to sit on the edge of the bed. She stepped back a couple of feet so he could get the best view of her entire enticing body. She began to take off her clothes. She was wearing a very tight pair of blue booty shorts and a white stretchy blouse that stopped below her breasts revealing her tight flat mid-section. She peeled off the shorts in a very playful manner revealing her very tiny white panties. You could see the imprint of her juicy coochie. His nature began to rise right in front of her. She giggled. Priscilla pulled off her blouse revealing a white push-up bra that could barely hold her bulging breasts. Greg was fixated on this moving picture of youth, beauty, and vibrant flawless skin. 'How could any woman's body be so perfect?' Greg thought as the push-up bra dropped effortlessly to the floor. Greg was not seeing some unnamed stripper girl. He was seeing a friend someone he knew and connected with. He was comfortable with this girl and Priscilla didn't look at Greg as a client, but rather as a friend that didn't judge her for her profession. He was a warm friend that appreciated her for who she is. She pushed him back onto the bed, slid the condom on him, and got up on top of him remembering how much he enjoyed that position the last time. "Ummm, how are you, Greg?" Priscilla asked. "Oh, I'm just fine," Greg answered. "I hope there is not trouble in Paradise," she said probing him trying to find out why they called her, "we who work at the club nickname this place 'Paradise.'" "Paradise, huh?" Greg replied trying to keep up with his younger sex partner, "You know Priscilla, there is always something." "Greg it's none of my business," She said while reversing her position, "but why would Cynthia call in a call girl when she is beautiful and sexy herself? You do find her attractive?" "Yes, very." Greg was moaning a little. "It's none of my business, but Greg, protect your heart." Priscilla encouraged him, "I worry about you." "That is so kind of you," Greg responded. "Ya know what I wish?" She started her confession. "What?" "I wish that one day you would call for me to come dance for you without her or anyone." Priscilla explained. "Why?" Greg was wondering. "Because it would be just me and you," She stated, "I wouldn't have to answer to your crazy girlfriend. I could just relax and enjoy being with you." "That is very sweet Priscilla," Greg admitted, "now I want to do something to you. Did you bring a corset?" "Boy, I thought you would never ask," Priscilla answered with a big Kool-Aid smile. "It's in my bag, and since I met you, I don't leave home without it." Greg helped her put it on and he made it very tight. "This is becoming our favorite position," Greg told his beautiful companion as he pulled her to the edge of the bed and spread her legs wide. "I want you to enjoy this." He started off slowly raising her enjoyment with each penetration. Greg had his energy this day. He was strong as a bull. He was determined to give this call girl the best sex of her lifetime. Priscilla was moaning deeply as her eyes rolled up into the back of her head. With Greg standing over her, she felt safe and secure. He pushed her further onto the bed and he leaned on her legs so he could position himself as deeply inside of her as he could go. "Oh! Ohhh!" Priscilla couldn't help but moan louder, "You don't ever need to pay me to have sex with you Greg! I never said this to anyone since I've been in this business." "Don't talk Babydoll," He told her, "I just want you to enjoy this and I just want you to remember this feeling. Ok?" "Ok," she replied, "I like when you call me Babydoll." "Ok then, that's my nickname for you and only you, Babydoll." Greg promised. Once Greg had her on her back, he was so distracted by her breasts. He grabbed some oil out of her bag that was next to the bed. "You don't mind if I . . ." Greg asked politely. "I love that, yeah, go ahead." She uttered catching her breath. Greg spread the oil all over her breasts caressing them gently. Her titties were absolutely flawless. They were tight and perky. He began playing with her nipples. Putting them in his mouth sucking them tenderly. That turned her own and before you knew it, she had rolled him over on his back and climbed up on him like a cowgirl at a rodeo show. These two love birds went back and forth, and back and forth. Greg was holding his own with this young energetic princess of the bedroom. Priscilla was pleased and surprised that this older dude was keeping up. He was really pleasing her. Priscilla thought to herself, 'I wish all my clients were like this.' When the two had finished their flaming hot sexual encounter, Priscilla told Greg something that he would never forget. "I could lose my job for this," She added, "but I'm giving you my personal cell number. Greg, call me when you need anything. If you have a party, if a couple of guys are getting together to watch the game, if it's a birthday, if you just want to play with my tits, or if you just want to be with me. I'll strip for you anytime Greg for free. I consider you my friend. I trust you." She wrote her number on a piece of paper and signed it 'Babydoll.'

Chapter Six
| The Big Challenge |

Cynthia knew she was still in the dog house with Greg. She needed to get his attention off her taking Tasha to Vegas. Friday was coming and the threesome decided to hang out at Cynthia's place again. It just seemed perfect for what they were doing. There was so much room and you had the staff there to cook for you. It was like a luxury hotel for free. From Greg's perspective, he didn't want Tasha to know that he was mad at Cynthia, so as not to upset the apple cart and keep the threesome going. Cynthia was aware of that dynamic also so she used it to her advantage. She told Tasha that they should have sex with everyone present. So, when Greg was having sex with Tasha, then Cynthia would be present and vice versa. She wanted Tasha to be present when she was doing it with Greg. That way Greg would have to perform well in front of Tasha, ensuring that Greg would have good sex with her. However, Cynthia needed to get this bad relationship with Greg off the table. She needed it to go away. Yet, Greg was still mad and he wasn't letting go of this easy. Therefore, Cynthia came up with a plan to take the spotlight off of this negative situation. She would announce her plan to the threesome on Saturday morning over breakfast. Greg was trying to figure out how he would get through Friday night. How he would get through a night of having sex with someone that he was mad at in front of his girl without her knowing.

Friday night after work, all three of them were there. They went upstairs to the master bedroom. Tasha was going to go first. She decided to do a little striptease for her man. She had gotten a brand new see-thru orange outfit for Greg. He loved it! Orange looks so good on Tasha and it turns Greg on because he knows she is doing it to please him. Once she was finally naked, Greg grabs her and throws her onto the bed. Cynthia wants to get involved so she says, "Tasha, let him taste your coochie." Greg goes down on Tasha. He is on his knees in the bed. He has Tasha's clit in his mouth and he is passing his tongue over it to arouse her. Meanwhile, Cynthia starts rubbing Greg's dick. Greg can't say anything and honestly, it does feel good, but he is still mad at Cynthia. He knows this is an effort to make him forget his anger. Cynthia kept involving herself in the love making Tasha and Greg were doing. This was bothersome to Greg, but he couldn't do anything about it in front of Tasha. Tasha was having a good time and enjoying the sex when Cynthia gave her a signal. At this point Tasha told him, "Greg, save some for Cynthia. It's her turn now. Make love to Cynthia." These are the words Greg didn't want to hear. Greg is good at avoidance behavior. So Greg says, "Ok, let me take a little break first." He went over to the intercom system and said, "Mrs. Rose, are you there?" "Yes, Master Greg." Rose responded. "Can you please make me a tall cup of your famous hot chocolate?" Greg asked politely. "Yes, coming right up." Rose announced. "I'll be down in a minute." Greg said. Cynthia dashed out of the room headed to the kitchen. She got some pills out of the cupboard and as soon as Rose had made the hot chocolate, Cynthia opened one of the pills pouring its content into Greg's hot chocolate with a sneaky smile on her face. She stirred the cup good. When Greg came down she told him, "Got to get changed baby. I'll meet you upstairs." She dashed out of the kitchen smiling so proud of herself. Rose saw the whole thing. "Trouble in Paradise?" Rose asked. "Mrs. Rose, I want to kill Cynthia." Greg admitted. "So, how do you make love to someone you are mad at?" Rose questioned him. "I don't know. It's disturbing." Greg confessed. "You should just be honest and tell Tasha." Rose detailed to Greg. "Yeah, you're right." Greg replied, "Maybe I should do that, but that would destroy everything." "Greg, it appears that everything is already destroyed." Rose commented. "Hmmm…, you may be right…, you may be right." Greg responded thoughtfully.

He drank his hot chocolate and made his way back upstairs. He saw Cynthia on the balcony. He went to her and grabbed her hand bringing her to the bed. Tasha, who was laying on the bed, was dosing off. Cynthia shook her leg to wake her. Tasha asked, "Am I in the way. Do I need me to move?" "You're fine," Cynthia said, "I just don't want you to miss the show." Cynthia was wearing a beautiful silk robe. Greg was sitting on the edge of the bed. Standing in front of him, Cynthia let the robe drop to the floor. She was completely nude, no bra, and no panties. Just baby brown soft skin. Yes, this was appealing to Greg even though he was mad. Nonetheless, there was something else going on inside of Greg's body. He was becoming quite horny and very aggressive. He doesn't know where this was coming from because he didn't feel like this when he made love to Tasha. "Come here girl," Greg boldly stated as aggression over took him. He flung her onto the bed and went at it. No foreplay at all; just deep penetrating thrusts like he was a beast. Cynthia was hanging on for dear life with that same sneaky smile she had in the kitchen. She knew what was happening. She knew the drug was kicking in. Greg changed position. He stood up and bent her over. He stood behind her and did it to her doggy style while holding her arms pulling her towards him with each thrust. This wasn't enough, so he grabbed her under the crease of her elbows to be able to pull her farther back with each penetration. It was a bit rough, but Cynthia didn't care. She just wanted Greg to enjoy her and forget his anger. "Don't stop, don't you stop," Cynthia encouraged Greg, "I know you want this. You love it." "My Goodness!!!" Tasha exclaimed, "What did you do to my boyfriend? He is going crazy on you girl. Cynthia you must tell me your secret. You bring out the animal in Greg." "Can't... talk... now...," Cynthia released to the rhythm of Greg's thrusts, "will... talk... later..." Cynthia's body was literally rocking, swaying, back, and forth. It was like she was on a powerful ride at the fair that just jerks you around. Greg put his arms under her legs, which were bent at the knees, he lifted her up so he could penetrate her warm pussy. He bounced her up and down while standing up. Cynthia was very happy. She won. He would forget his anger and enjoy this incredible sexual experience they were sharing together. Normally, Cynthia would not be excited about having rough sex. It's not really her thing. However, tonight was an exception. The harder the better. This meant the man she loved was having a good time. He was having her as an entrée; a very spicey hot entrée. "Baby, are you hurting Cynthia?" Tasha asked worried. "No Tasha. I'm fine." Cynthia reassured her, "I'm fine. Let's just let him go and see how far this animal can go." He threw her on the bed on her stomach, and slid it up into her from the back. "Uhhh," she moaned, "that feels so good. Keep it coming babe." Greg kept going and going until he couldn't go anymore. Cynthia was worn out completely. She had never been happier. This was the first step in getting things back to normal between her and Greg. After this great expenditure of energy, Greg dozed off quickly. The three of them all fell asleep in the same bed for the first time.

The next morning, Cynthia woke up first and went downstairs. Tasha also woke up and went downstairs. Greg was still sleeping so Cynthia headed back upstairs to wake him. "Rise and shine," She greeted, "the early bird gets the worm." "Oh," Greg moaned, "my head hurts." "I will get you an aspirin babe." Cynthia told him, "By the way, thanks for last night. You went into beast mode on me." "Yeah, I don't know what that was all about." Greg responded. "I think it was about my boyfriend unconsciously forgiving me." Cynthia suggested. "Really?" Greg muttered. "Really." She replied smiling. They both went down stairs for breakfast. "Master Greg," Rose asked, "how are you this morning?" "A little headache," Greg expressed, "but otherwise I'm fine." "Today we are serving salmon patties, eggs, bacon, sausage, hash browns, and exquisite French Toast with cinnamon." Rose announced professionally. As the threesome ate together, Cynthia began to explain the Big Challenge. "We are going have some fun this weekend." Cynthia explained, "We will have a contest that everyone is going to enjoy. This Sunday there is a music festival in Hotlanta. Everyone is going to be there. Greg, there will be an ample supply of sexy, hot women of all types and ages. Tasha for you and I, there will be an abundance of gorgeous men that might find us very attractive. The contest is simple: the person that gets the most telephone numbers win. These numbers will have to be verified. We will have Rose call the numbers to make sure the person spoke with you. You will have two hours to get the numbers from 12 noon to 2pm." "Cynthia, are you kidding?" Greg asked, "I thought you said this was a contest. This is a blowout. There is no way that both of you combined could get more numbers than me in one-half the time." "Oh yeah… the male ego." Cynthia replied, "Men are better at hunting than woman. Men are better at everything than women. Greg, I thought you were more evolved than this." "No, that is not what I said," Greg replied, "I wasn't talking about men in general. I was talking about me. Ok, you are telling me that I can lie and get as many telephone numbers as possible. Then how can I lose?" "I can get more numbers than you. That's how you can lose." Cynthia answered. "No, you can't." Greg was serious. "What are the consequences if you lose?" Tasha asked. "Greg will give the consequences for the girls if they lose. Tasha and I will give the consequences if Greg loses; when Greg loses." Cynthia announced with a smile. "Buck naked," Greg specified, "I got some guys coming over Sunday to watch some football from 6pm-10pm. You girls will host this party completely naked. The guys can slap that ass, squeeze those titties, and take pictures with you to capture the moment. The only requirement for you girls is that you be gracious naked hostesses and provide an erotic dance at half-time to entertain the guys while they record the video." "That's terrible," Cynthia admitted, "but it will never happen to us." "What bad thing can we think up for Greg Cynthia?" Tasha asked. "That's easy," Cynthia added, "we will have our dear friend Greg become a member of the male strippers and record the event for posterity." The girls both laughed. "The thought of Tasha being subjected to male scrutiny while she is naked doesn't sit right with me," Greg confessed, "so I would like to create a clause in this contest to protect anyone who can see they are going to lose. We turn in our names and numbers on the hour. At 1pm when we both turn in our names and numbers, we will clearly see who is ahead. At that point, you two can bow out to avoid the humiliating naked hostess situation. However, if you stay in and continue to get numbers, you will suffer the consequences. The outcome, whatever it is, is unchangeable." "Ok, your 'escape being a naked hostess clause' is duly noted and accepted." Cynthia confirmed. "We will all leave Paradise together, arrive at the event together, and start at the same time." Cynthia told everyone. "Rose will set up a table at the event. We will call the location Ground Zero. Ground Zero is where you must come to give her the telephone numbers you collected. This way she can verifying them at that time." Greg's anger was turning into revenge. He just wanted

Cynthia to become the naked hostess. It would serve her right and maybe then she would see why what she did was so wrong. Maybe not, but still revenge would be fun. Greg made a phone call while he was sitting there at the table in order to scare the girls. "Dude, whatup?" Greg saluted, "We still on for football at my place Sunday evening, right?" "Yeah, tell Terrance and Jo-jo not to be late," Greg announced with a big smile, "because I got some honeys to host our football party." "You heard me right the first time," Greg replied forcefully, "fine honeys. I'm talking 'bout big booties and fat titties and slender waist lines." "No, no, no, man," Greg continued, "hear me out. I ain't got to the best part yet. These girls are going to be buck naked!! Buck naked!!! Did I studder?" "No, they fine," Greg reassured Nate, "Nate, have I ever let you down?" "Ok that one time," Greg admitted, "but I'm going to redeem myself this time. Plus you don't have to pay these dimes a penny. We are getting this totally free of charge. So, bring your cell phone to take pictures and video. And get ready to slap some ass every time they walk by saying, 'Would you like some dip with your chips?'" "Ok bruh," Greg told him, "be there or be square. Peace out." Cynthia looked disgusted. She said, "Your friends sound like dogs." "Are you getting scared?" Greg asked, "Is it becoming a reality to you now? Can you see yourself naked and humiliated while these dogs take your picture and make sexually explicit videos of you? Cynthia, you got too much at stake here. It will be better if you dropped out of this contest." "He's good with girls," Tasha confirmed, "he's always been good with girls, maybe we should . . ." Cynthia cut her off,

"...Don't even say it. He's trying to divide us and make us scared before we even start the contest. You have to stick with me. It's girls against the boys. Man against woman." "Ok, I'm going to make it even easier for you two." Greg offered an idea with a confident smile, "We are going to add all the girl's numbers together and I will still win. Two against one. Just to make it fair. Ya'll get your little sexy dance together. Better start practicing now." "You are on!" Cynthia said, "You are so on!!" "Girl, we bet' not lose." Tasha was a little nervous because the stakes were too high. "Don't worry, don't worry. We got this." Cynthia reassured Tasha. Greg told the ladies he was going to get started on his plan to get the most numbers. Tasha said she would hang out with Cynthia so they could get their plan together. Greg left.

"What are we going to do to win?" Tasha asked. Cynthia grabbed her hand and the girls headed up to the bedroom talking all the way. "Oh no, Tash. It's going to have to be shorter than that. You got some beautiful thick legs. It's time you put them on display. Let's find something even sexier for you to wear." She took that skirt off and tried on another one. "Look, we don't have time to develop some long conversation with these guys. We got to get in and get out quickly." Cynthia explained. "So, once you get the number, girl you got to go." "I got it," Tasha replied, "but I hope I don't run into anyone that I know. I don't want them to think I'm a hoe with this mini, mini skirt on." They laughed together as they were having fun preparing for the contest. However, Tasha was genuinely afraid of getting beat by Greg. When Sunday, came Greg showed up at Paradise with his boy Nate (The guy he was talking to on the phone about the football party with the naked hostesses). Nate was driving his black van. Greg had put a magnetic sticker on the side. It was the Sport's Illustrated logo. Cynthia saw the van with the logo and asked, "Your friend works for Sports Illustrated?" "No," Greg told her, "I work for Sports Illustrated; at least for today. See my badge?" He showed her his fake Sports Illustrated ID badge. "You are such a liar." Cynthia responded. "Like shooting fish in a barrel," Greg acknowledged, "this is going to be too easy." Nate stepped out of the van, saluted, and stood at attention. "Lieutenant Colonel Nathaniel Bridges reporting for coochie sir, I mean duty." Nate announced loudly. Greg busted out laughing, "That was awesome," he told him, "reporting for coochie instead of reporting for duty. Soldier, I've learned that sometimes coochie is duty." He continued laughing. These two guys were having too much fun and the contest hadn't even started. "My job is to help my boy." Nate said, "I'm here to pick out the finest honeys on the scene and direct Greg to them. Have I died and gone to heaven? Apparently. It's my job to pick out the girls with the tightest skirts on, with the shortest shorts on, and with the biggest most succulent breasts. Most of all, the girls with the sexiest booties. Only a qualified soldier like myself could handle an assignment like this." Once Tasha and Cynthia saw the plan that Greg had to get the girls numbers, they were a bit scared. "Girl, I don't know," Tasha told Cynthia feeling a bit apprehensive, "I don't want to be a naked hostess." "This is theory." Cynthia explained, "Let's see it put into action. Can it really work? These women in Atlanta are not that dumb. Don't give up yet." Tasha and Cynthia got into the limo with Rose. All the participants in the contest left Paradise at the same time and went to the event together.

Rose set up ground zero next to the sidewalk. It was 5 minutes before gametime. "Any second thoughts girls?" Greg was smiling, "Now is the time. Trust me you don't want to be the sexiest naked hostesses in Hotlanta do you?" He laughed. "Don't listen to him Tash," Cynthia said, "nobody is going for your little scam. Women are too smart. Cause all you are doing is appealing to a woman's vanity telling her she is beautiful enough to be a swimsuit model. Girls in this city are not going for that. I can tell you right now." Greg was just laughing his head off. He couldn't even make up a reply to that because Cynthia's counter argument was Greg's original premise. A beautiful woman would give up her telephone number for a shot at being in the Sports Illustrated swimsuit edition. Rose announced, "On your mark, get ready, Go!" Greg yelled, "Let the games begin!" "I got two of them over here for you right now. I'm on the case." Nate said. "Dude," Greg replied, "you are the man. These are two lovely specimens if I have to say so myself." Greg walked over to the beautiful ladies and started his spill. "Hello ladies." Greg started out politely, "My name is Gerald Martin. I work for Sports Illustrated. I'm in the swimsuit department. Do you have a moment?" "Sure." She answered. "What is your name and your friend's name?" "I'm Candice and this is Liza." "Pleased to meet both of you. Have you ever thought about modeling?" Greg asked.

"Well, I don't know." She replied. "Both of you are rare beauties. Just what my company is looking for." Greg explained, "I'm taking pictures of lovely young ladies to send to my company for a chance to be in the swimsuit issue of my magazine. Do you mind if I take pictures of your two?" Greg whips out his camera and snaps a pictures of the two girls. "Let's see what you're working with here. Could I get you to turn around, yeah, you know the drill. Excellent." "Can we get a close-up? We need to see those beautiful eyes." Greg stated being smooth with his words. "Ok, if you could give me your name and number, I will have someone from my company verify that you did give us permission to submit your picture. You know for legal purposes. Here is my card."

The girls were more than willing to give up their numbers. Nate and Greg walked down a little further and continued their little scam. They didn't have anyone tell them no. Every woman they approached gave Greg their telephone number; every single one. And mind you, they only approached the most beautiful women. Nate and Greg were having too much fun. Meanwhile, the girls were not doing as well. They were able to meet guys and get some Numbers, but it was slow. After they got the number, the guys were trying to take them out, trying to walk around the park with them, they wanted to show the girls their crib, or their car. So, Tasha and Cynthia's problem was they could get the number, but then it was hard to get away from the dudes fast enough to keep up with Nate and Greg. Who were getting 2 and 3 numbers at a time. Spending less than 5 mins with each set of girls. After the first hour, Greg had

28 numbers. He went back to ground zero and gave those numbers to Rose to start verifying. Tasha and Cynthia had 9 numbers. Greg looked Tasha in the eyes and told her seriously, "Baby, you can't win. It is time for you to give up and opt out of this contest. If you continue, you will be a naked hostess in exactly 5 hours. Remember the rules. The outcome is irreversible. It is unchangeable." Tasha was scared. She looked at her home girl Cynthia and told her, "I can't just have no strange man feeling on me and taking naked videos of me. Girl, I was not raised like that. You should join me right now Cynthia." "Never, it is not over," Cynthia said, "I can still win. Greg will never beat me." "Wow, wow, you can't make this stuff up." Greg stated in disbelief, "You can't believe this. Her pride has blinded her mind. Cynthia is a logical, intelligent, and a rational person entrusted with the ownership a of a huge corporation. On a daily basis she has to make hard decisions. Decisions that affect the lives of several hundred of the company's employees, the board of directors, and many, many shareholders. Yet, she is so blind, being full of her own pride she can't see the inevitable when the writing is on the wall. Nine to twenty-eight in one hour. Come on man, anyone can see that." "Men are not better than women," Cynthia repeated again, "I can still win, Greg will never beat me." "Ok Mrs. Naked Hostess, I tried." Greg said, "Back to work Nate. Find me some sexy, juicy, hot women, and lots of them!" "Sir, yes sir!" Nate blurted out standing at attention like a soldier. The contest continued, but you had to feel sorry for Cynthia. She had lost it. There was no way that she

could catch Greg. She was going to lose. Greg and Nate ended up with another 30 names and numbers for a grand total of 58. Cynthia received 5 more in the last hour for a total of 14. Rose verified over 35 names so Greg told her that was enough, "My 35 verified still beats her 14. This game is over."

The whole crew went back to Paradise. Cynthia was steaming. Once inside the house Greg spoke to her, "I tried to warn you Cynthia, but you wouldn't listen." Cynthia didn't say a word. She gave Greg a look that would kill. Fire was shooting from her eyes. "Come on," Greg said, "say something." "I don't want strange men touching me," Cynthia confessed. "So, you want to back out now?" Greg replied. "Why didn't you back out at 1pm today?" "No Miss Prissy, I want you to suffer humiliation." Greg openly admitted, "It might teach you something. You are not backing out." "Ok," Cynthia responded, "if I say that I was wrong, would you let me off the hook?" "No." Greg answered with no mercy. "This has nothing to do with this contest." Cynthia told everyone. "Watch it Ms. Heart," Greg suggested seriously, "measure your next words carefully." He was staring right into her eyes. "Oh, come on Greg," Cynthia said, "just let me off the hook this one time. I'll make it up to you I promise." "Hmmmm..., no." Greg repeated. Cynthia walked up to him and whispered in his ear, "I will suck your dick for hours and give you so much wet pussy. Not just mine, but Priscilla's and Tatianna's. Whoever's you desire. I will worship you." "No." Greg was inflexible. Now Cynthia was 95 hot! Not only had Greg won, but he wasn't budging. So, in psychology if positive reinforcement doesn't work try negative reinforcement. "I need to speak to you in private," Cynthia told him, "Tasha, we will be right back." Cynthia led him to the back bedroom on the main floor. She closed the door. "Ok, I need you to show me a little mercy." Cynthia explained, "If you show me some mercy, I will show you some mercy." "I'm listening." Greg replied emotionless. "Your little friend Priscilla will be fired before 6 pm today." Cynthia boasted. "Why? How? It makes no sense." Greg was visibly disturbed. "There are no secrets in Paradise Greg," Cynthia pointed out, "I know she gave you her personal cell number. That is a firing offense." "Really, you would blackmail me?" Greg asked, "I don't believe this. You just offered me worship and as much wet pussy as I could possibly want. Then the next thing is to ruin an innocent girl's life just to get what you want." "Just to avoid what I don't want." Cynthia corrected him. "Well," she said, "do we have a deal?" Greg paused. He had almost beaten her, but he couldn't let her hurt Priscilla. She had nothing to do with any of this. "Ok, we have a deal." Greg muttered reluctantly. "I'm still gonna give you the pussy Greg," Cynthia promised, "Tell Tasha we came to an agreement. I will contact the club and let them send Priscilla and Tatianna to your place to be the naked hostesses in place of Tasha and I." "No, I will contact the club," Greg added, "I want her to be working for me, agreed?" "Agreed." She answered relieved she solved this problem. Greg was still a little salty, but he explained to Tasha they worked it out and would have the strippers be the naked hostesses. "I got to get home so I can catch the game," Greg said with a big smile.

After this historic football party, Greg was a superhero to his friends. Nate had to give Greg his props. The party was one to brag about for years to come. This party will become legendary among men. "Greg, I don't know how you pulled it off." Nate divulged as he gave Greg a fist bump smiling, "Those were the most beautiful naked hostesses I've ever seen, and I have the videos to prove it. You are the man!" Greg threw up his hands with double peace signs saying, "Yes sir." They both laughed.

Chapter Seven
| Vegas Baby!! |

"Jessica, I need you to come over here right now," Cynthia told her, "I can't talk about it over the phone." "Ok, I'm on the way." Jessica answered. Once Jessica arrived at Paradise, Cynthia invited her in. They sat down in the living room. "I just received this letter," Cynthia handed the letter to Jessica, "It's about the party." Jessica read the letter in horror. There was a thumb drive in the envelope. "Did you look at what was on the thumb drive?" Jessica asked. "Ah, yeah," Cynthia replied, "not good. Not good at all. Let me show you." There was a computer in the corner of the room, they went over to the computer, attached the thumb drive, and accessed the file. It was a video clip. Cynthia played the clip. It was one of the male strippers having sex with Jessica. She was bent over topless. Her face and naked body were seen clearly in the video as the stripper was doing it to her from behind doggy style. "My God," Jessica released horrified, "this will ruin my marriage if this gets out." "That's why I couldn't take a chance of speaking with you about this over the phone." Cynthia shared. "What am I going to do?" Jessica asked. "Well, they explained in the letter that we can't involve the police." Cynthia replied, "The less people know about this the better, I think." "Of course." Jessica agreed. "Jessica, there is one very good thing," Cynthia explained, "they only asked for $50,000 dollars. They don't know who you are. These are amateurs. They didn't target you. They don't know what they are doing. You and your husband are worth over 600 million dollars and all they asked for was $50,000 dollars. That tells you everything." "Yeah, you are right. These are amateurs," Jessica noted. "I think we should just give them the money and make this thing go away." Cynthia suggested, "Don't involve the police or investigators, don't draw any attention to this thing. And above all, we must make sure your husband does not find out about this indiscretion. I know everyone got wild at that party, and everyone was drinking, but I never thought something like this would happen." "The letter says he will make contact with us via telephone 9pm tonight." Jessica stated. "Yeah, he has my home number," Cynthia detailed, "he will call here at 9pm and we will be ready. I will take the call and you can listen in on the other line. I think we should do what he asks and get them the money. What do you think?" "Absolutely Cynthia," Jessica agreed looking afraid, "I need this to go away fast." "Ok, that's the plan." Cynthia responded. "Can you get the money?" "Let me go to the bank before it closes," Jessica suggested, "I can get the cash." "No, they may request it in smaller bills," Cynthia countered, "so just wait and see what they request. They have to be reasonable and give you the time to get the money. I'm guessing they will allow you to get the money out of the bank tomorrow and deliver it to them tomorrow. So just sit tight and we will see what they say."

At 9pm the phone rang. "Hello." Cynthia answered. "50 thousand in 100's and 50's only by 9pm tomorrow or this video goes viral." A distorted voice at the other end of the line declared.

"Where?" Cynthia asked. "We will contact you at this number tomorrow at 6pm. No police. No dye. No funny business or the video goes public." Click! The line went dead. "Ok, it sounds simple enough." Cynthia stated, "Half of the 50 thousand in 100 dollar bills and the other half in fifty dollar bills. That's 250 one-hundred-dollar bills and 500 fifty-dollar bills. That's a grand total of 750 individual bills. That amount of cash will fit in a small bag easily. Can you get the money tomorrow?" "Yes. I will go to the bank first thing in the morning." Jessica expressed. "Good." Cynthia said, "After that discreetly bring the money to my place and stay here with me until the call at 6pm. Then we will deliver the cash wherever they tell us, and that should be the end of this. Don't tell anyone anything. Got it?" "Got it." Jessica agreed.

Tasha and Greg didn't know about Jessica being blackmailed. At 6pm the phone rang like clockwork. "Hello," Cynthia said. "Do you have the money?" A distorted voice asked. "Yes, yes." Cynthia responded eagerly. "Ok, there is a park about 5 blocks north of your house. Do you know this place?" "Yes of course." Cynthia answered. "On the north end of the park there is a fountain. Directly in front of the fountain is a bench. At 9pm place the bag of money under the bench, out of sight, and leave. No police. No funny business and there will be no problems. Once we have the money, we will send the original video recording to you via post. Got it?" "Got it." Cynthia responded. Click! The line went dead. "Ok," Cynthia told Jessica, "I will do it. I will place the bag under the bench." "Why you?" Jessica asked. "Because Jessica, this is all my fault," Cynthia lamented, "I shouldn't have gotten everyone drunk. I should have paid better attention to those strippers. I believe they are behind this. So let me do it. I'm not putting you in any more danger." "I'm going in the car with you." Jessica insisted. "Ok."

It was almost 9pm and it was dark. Jessica and Cynthia arrived at the park. "There is the fountain," Cynthia said, "stay here I'll be back in a minute." Jessica watched as Cynthia walked to the bench, sat down, and set her big bag next to the bench. She calmly reached into the big bag, pulled out a smaller bag of money, and quickly placed it under the bench. She got up and left, taking only her big bag with her walking away very quickly. When she got back to the car she told Jessica, "Let's get out of here right now." They drove off and went back to Paradise. "Everything went off perfectly," Cynthia reassured her, "there should be no problems. We did just what he asked. No funny business." "I hope he keeps his word." Jessica responded. "He will." Cynthia reassured her. After this talk Jessica went home. After Jessica left Paradise, Cynthia took her car and went back to the park. She walked over to the bench and got the money. This whole thing had been set up by Cynthia to pay for her trip to Vegas. Nobody knew.

The time had finally come for the girl's trip to Vegas. Tasha was so jazzed. "Greg, can you come by and check on my place while I'm gone?" Tasha asked. "Absolutely baby." Greg replied. "So, when do you leave and how long will you guys be gone?" "Here is our schedule," Tasha said excited, "we leave on Tuesday morning at 10am. We will be there from Tuesday through the following

Thursday. We return on Thursday night at 8:30pm." "You going to work on Friday?" Greg asked. "Not a chance," Tasha answered, "I took it off too. Baby I'm gonna miss you so much. So you better be ready when I get back on Thursday night." "I'll be here and I will be ready for you." Greg promised, "Don't think about me. Have a good time and don't do anything I wouldn't do." They both laughed.

Cynthia telephoned Greg sometime later. "Greg, how are you?" Cynthia asked sincerely. "I'm good, I'm good." Greg replied. "Look Greg, I'm not leaving you here in Atlanta alone." Cynthia explained, "I remember my promise to you and have set everything up for you. Tuesday, after you get off from work, I want you to go to Paradise. My whole plan for you and your pleasure will be explained to you at that time. So just go to Paradise on Tuesday after you get off work." "What are you planning?" Greg curiously asked. "It is a surprise just for you from me." Cynthia told him, "Enjoy your time while we are gone." 'Hmmm, what am I getting myself into?' Greg thought. Greg did feel a little left out. He wasn't as mad at Cynthia as before, however, he didn't trust her. He was always on his guard with her.

Greg took Tuesday morning off to drive the girls to the airport. "I can't believe you girls are only taking one carry-on bag each on the flight." Greg said in disbelief, "You girls are going to be gone nine days." "This way we don't have to wait for our bags when we arrive in Vegas." Cynthia replied, "Greg we hit the ground running." "Ok then, what are you going to wear for 9 days?" Greg asked again curiously. "We are going shopping Greg," Tasha declared, "it's all part of the master plan." "Greg, don't you worry about us." Cynthia told him. Tasha got out of the car to open the hatch back and grab the bags. Then Cynthia whispered to Greg, "Just make sure you're at Paradise after work." She smiled. They both hugged and kissed Greg goodbye as they hurried to catch their flight to Vegas. Greg told Tasha, "Call me when you land safely."

Cynthia and Tasha flew first class. It was the first time for Tasha. She loved it because she loves being pampered. Flight time was 4 hours and 17 minutes. That time would fly by because the girls would be talking and making plans. "Tasha," Cynthia said while on the plane, "we got 50 thousand dollars to spend in Vegas together girl." "What?" Tasha asked in true surprise. "That's right," Cynthia reassured her, "and we can't go back to Hotlanta without spending all of it. So that means only the finest for us. That also means we are going to be shopping our asses off girl. I got some male strippers coming Thursday night. Only the best ones. The most expensive ones. The ones with the biggest packages. They are going to give you and I a private party. Remember what happens in Vegas stays in Vegas. I waited until we got on the plane to tell you this, so you can't tell Greg about our scandalous plans." "Girl you are sooo bad." Tasha said smiling. "You know Tash," Cynthia replied, "sometimes it's good to be bad." They both laughed. A good feeling came over both of them. They were going to have a very good time.

Around 2:35 Atlanta time, Greg received a call from Tasha. The girls had landed safely in Vegas. They talked for a couple of minutes. Greg told her to have a blast and stay out of trouble. "Keep a close eye on your partner in crime," Greg told Tasha, "she can be a little tricky." "Tricky and fun," Tasha replied, "but don't you worry I got this." "Ok, love you," Greg responded, "good bye Tasha." Cynthia and Tasha checked into their luxury suite room at The Venetian Hotel. This room was spectacular. Tasha told Cynthia, "Girlfriend, I could get used to this."

Greg was getting off from work and heading over to Paradise. 'What could this girl have in mind for me?' He thought. He knew it would be something crazy, and he was sure this for certain. He pulled up to Cynthia's place and rang the bell. Rose opened the door, "Ah, Master Greg," she greeted him warmly, "we have been awaiting your arrival." "We?" Greg asked being surprised. "Right this way." Rose said as she led him to the living room. There was a lady waiting there for him. She had on a lovely white dress with flowers on it. Oh my! Greg did recognize the young lady. Why it was Priscilla from the club, but she wasn't dressed hot or sexy. So maybe she wasn't there for his pleasure. Greg was a bit confused. He tilted his head sideways and smiled at his beautiful friend. "Hi, Greg," Priscilla said smiling back at him, "you're probably a little surprised to see me. Right?" "A little," Greg responded, "but I'm glad to see you. So, what is going on here?" "Ok, let me explain." Priscilla started out, "Cynthia has given me the assignment to be your date, or escort, for the time she and Tasha are in Vegas. She doesn't want to leave you alone, and she wants to make sure you have everything you need specifically, and I quote, 'Make sure he has everything he would have if Tasha and I were there.' end of quote." Greg laughed under his breath. "Well, then you will be hanging with me, right?" "Morning, noon, and night," Priscilla assured him, "we are joined at the hip." "Ok, that's not too bad," Greg responded, "I look forward to hanging with my friend." Priscilla's face lit up. She gave Greg an enthusiastic bright ear to ear smile for saying something so sweet about her. However, after a couple of seconds, the smile evaporated from her face. "Oh no," Greg cringed, "there's more isn't there?" "Yes," Priscilla sighed, "there's two more things." "Just two?" Greg was being sarcastic. Priscilla nodded towards the kitchen. Greg swung his head towards the kitchen. Two of the sexiest young models came around the corner and entered the living room. "Angel and Tatianna!" Greg announced surprised again, "Where did you girls come from?" Tatianna and Angel were dressed in their usual sexy attire. They had on matching see thru baby doll outfits, pink and light blue. He turned his attention back to Priscilla for an explanation. Priscilla got up and walked over to Greg. She whispered so only he could hear what she was saying. He could tell she was embarrassed by what she had to tell him. "You got to have sex with these girls," She whispered to him, "or I don't get paid for spending all this time with you." "Ok." Greg replied. "There's more." Priscilla whispered. "I thought you said 2 things," Greg asked, "Angel and Tatianna? That's 2 things, right?" "Angel and Tatianna is one thing," She responded, "there is one more thing." "Ok, hit me with it." Greg said a little annoyed by this whole thing. "I just need you to do something for me." Priscilla whispered. "What?" Greg asked. Rose walked in from the kitchen with a glass of juice and handed it to Greg. "Can you drink this?" Priscilla asked afraid he would say no. "Priscilla, what is in this drink?" Greg asked looking her directly in the eyes, "Don't lie to me. Don't lie for Cynthia. You are my trusted friend." "There is some type of drug in it that will make you more sexually aggressive." Priscilla explained. "It won't hurt you. Maybe give you a little headache later. It only lasts for 3 hours. It's also part of the deal." "So, you need me to drink this, huh?" Greg asked. "I'm so sorry Greg. Cynthia is bad sometimes, huh?" Priscilla noted. "Yeah, sometimes she is horrible." Greg said. He knew what was in that drink. He remembered that night of wild sex with Cynthia and the headache the next morning. He thought to himself, 'I was probably going to have sex with those girls anyway. This way I will show them a crazy good time and take care of my friend Priscilla.' He whispered to Priscilla, "Exactly how much is she paying you?" She hesitated, "She's paying me well, very well." "How much?" Greg insisted. Priscilla whispered, "25 thousand." "Wow!" Greg exclaimed. "Ok, I got this." He drank about half the glass of juice in one swallow. "Ladies, right this way," he directed.

Angel and Tatianna stripped down to their panties after they got inside the bedroom. Greg could feel the drug kicking in at that moment. He got up and put his arms around both girls. He led them to the mirror on the dresser. He oiled up both his hands with coconut oil. Standing behind them, he reached his hand around their bodies and slid his hands down into their panties. The sexy girls were looking in the mirror as Greg began to rub their pussies at the same time. It was slippery and warm. Up and down. Up and down. He rubbed them over and over again making sure to gently stimulate the clit on each girl. The girls started to squirm with pleasure. By the expressions on their faces, you could see Greg was getting to them. "Girls pump it back and forth." Greg commanded the young girls, "Back and forth girls." Greg had 'em going. They were sexually exciting themselves with this motion simultaneously. "Now, let's go round and round ladies," Greg encouraged them, "I know you can do it. Round and round. Do you feel my slippery hands on your warm cha-cha?" "Yes," "Yes," The two girls said breathlessly. "No, no, no, don't stop girls," Greg continued, "I didn't tell you to stop, did I? Now do it in unison." Greg encouraged the young and willing participants, "I want you to rotate that coochie in unison with your girlfriend." The girls were naturally good at this. They were professional exotic dancers. They began to rotate their hips in perfect synchronicity; in perfect timing. It was an amazing sight to see. Greg could feel the wetness on his fingers. Angel was about to explode. She was ready to go.

Greg was feeling aggressive from the drug. He slipped his finger between the lips of her tenderness and gently pulled Angel into the shower with him. He adjusted the temperature of the water so that it was warm. While he was adjusting the temperature of the water, he asked Angel to do her little trick of putting the condom on with no hands. She happily obliged. He began to soap his hands up good and rub her down tenderly. He stood behind her and soaped her naked breasts up as the warm water ran down her glorious young body. Greg turned the blonde princess towards him. He put one of his arms under her knee and lifted her leg up. Now she was standing on one leg on her tippy toes. She had to put her arms around Greg's neck to keep her balance. She needed him or she would fall. Greg slid his manhood between the lips of her wet dripping tenderness and began to thrust upward over and over again. Angel loved it. She was not in control. She was being penetrated by a man that had taken control of her senses, her body, and her pussy. The warm water was soothing. The steam was rising and filling the shower. The position she was in was rare to her. It was titillating. Angel loved the way Greg made love to her. She let go as Greg aggressively took her over. Poor Tatianna, she was sexually aroused by Greg playing with her coochie earlier, but felt let down when Greg took Angel into the shower. Tatianna had to wait, but she was his next target.

Greg finished satisfying Angel in the shower and turned his attention to Tatianna. Greg dried off and changed his condom. He took Tatianna hands and had her stand up. She had been sitting on the bed waiting for him previously. Tatianna had the lightest most beautiful blue eyes. These radiant eyes were staring at Greg as he slid her baby blue panties to the floor. Greg gently laid her on the bed, he got the coconut oil, and began to spread it over her body. He began to massage her. First her shoulders. Then her breasts. He held her breasts in such a manner that his thumbs were rubbing against her slippery nipples. Greg took his time to get

Tatianna aroused again. He started rubbing the oil on her tight stomach area getting ever so close to her clit with each pass. Greg's thumb gently massaged her clit, occasionally rubbing the entire length of the pussy with warm oil. He put his tongue on the lips of her tenderness licking it from the bottom to the top. Her back arched. She felt that. She liked that. It was time for Greg to make his move. He took Tatianna's feet and put them over his shoulders. He leaned forward putting his weight on her thighs. He was trying to position himself so that he could do two things at one time. He wanted to stimulate both the inside and the outside of her pussy at the same time. Greg was trying to slide it inside of her and rub the outside of her clit at the same time. To do this you must get the proper angle. It's trial and error until you master this art and learn the correct angle. Greg tried and tried, and soon enough he got it. He was penetrating her inside and outside with one thrust. He kept doing it and Tatianna kept getting hotter and hotter until she climaxed. She orgasmed in front of Angel and Priscilla. The girls recognized it immediately. Priscilla felt a little left out. It bothered her the most since she felt especially close to Greg. Angel was impressed because never had a client tried to please a call girl. This was an historic event that would be talked about among the all the call girls. Really, who wouldn't want to reach orgasm and get paid for it? It just happened for the first time for anyone in this strip club. Tatianna was the first.

Later, while Priscilla and Greg were in the car traveling to Greg's house, Priscilla opened up to Greg about that evening. "Greg, wow.

You were very aggressive with the girls." Priscilla said, "No one can believe you actually made Tatianna climax in orgasm. She will never stop talking about it. Greg you are really good with women. Most guys just want to fuck. They just want to get their dicks off and roll over. But that is not how you are. You care when you make love; even when you are aggressive. Why is that?" "I don't know," Greg said in deep thought, "Priscilla, I believe you get back whatever you give. Maybe not every single time, but generally. So always treat people like you want to be treated." "I have to confess something else. I was a little jealous of Tatianna." Priscilla informed him, "I wished it was me that you made climax instead of her." "Wow, thanks for being honest." Greg was a bit surprised. "Anyway, who knows what is going to happen?" Priscilla smiled and looked at Greg while he was driving. He was smiling too.

Meanwhile, Cynthia and Tasha were having a blast in Vegas. The first day they walked the strip to show Tasha all the huge beautiful hotels. Of course Cynthia knew all the hot spots to shop at. They were scheduled to see a show that night so they needed the appropriate dresses for the occasion. They purchased 2 beautiful dresses which were both similar in appearance. Cynthia's was red and Tasha's was blue. They took the dresses back to their room where they would put them on before going to the show. While in their room getting prepared to go, Cynthia wanted to know how things were going with Greg and his date. Therefore, she pulled up the video feed from her home on her cell. Cynthia had access to all the cameras in her house. She pulled up the video from the back bedroom where Greg was with Angel and Tatianna. Cynthia was watching that video when Tasha caught her off guard and asked her what she was looking at on the phone. Cynthia tried to switch to another room quickly so Tasha wouldn't see Greg in bed with Tatianna. In her haste she switched it to the upstairs bedroom showing the video of Jessica having sex with the male stripper. Tasha saw that video. "Oh, my goodness," Tasha exclaimed, "Jessica had sex with one of the male strippers." "Yeah girl, it was a huge scandal." Cynthia reported, "she was blackmailed for 50 thousand dollars because of it." "What?" Tasha asked being surprised, "Why didn't you tell me?" "No, we had to keep it quiet." Cynthia confessed, "We told no one. Jessica paid the guys off and made it go away very quietly. You know she is filthy rich, She and her husband are worth around 600 million." "Well, I'm glad everything turned out well for her." Tasha commented. The girls finished getting ready and went to the show in their stunning dresses.

Once Greg got Priscilla to his place, he could tell there was still something bothering her. "You ok?" Greg asked. "You seem like there is something on your mind. You can talk to me." "There is one more thing that Cynthia wants me to do," Priscilla admitted, "I was going to try to do it, but I can't. I respect you and Tasha too much. She wants me to disrespect Tasha by having sex with you in her bed. It is part of the deal." "Prisicilla, how would she know if you had sex with me in Tasha's bed?" Greg wondered feeling confused. "She left some red panties under Tasha's bed," Priscilla replied,

"I'm supposed to get those panties as proof that I was there and had sex with you in Tasha's bed." "Wow, you can't make this stuff up," Greg said being blown away by this information, "and think about this. Right now as we speak, she is on vacation with Tasha as her very best friend ever. The duplicity is mind-blowing." Greg thought for a moment then turned to Priscilla. "Babydoll, thanks for telling me the truth." Greg gratefully expressed, "We can fix this situation so that you get paid and I don't have to disrespect my girlfriend. It's simple. We just go over to Tasha's place and get the red panties from under the mattress. You can tell her you had sex with me in Tasha's bed and she will be none the wiser." "Greg you are the best." Priscilla responded, "Of course, I want to make the money, but I don't want to lose your friendship doing it." "I will swing by there tomorrow and get the panties." Greg informed. "Hopefully, that's everything." "Yes," Priscilla said sweetly, "that's everything."

The next morning Greg woke up to the smell of breakfast being cooked. He smelled bacon, sausage, grits, and eggs. It was weird because he didn't have all those ingredients in his refrigerator. He pulled himself out of bed and stumbled to the kitchen. Where he saw Priscilla. She wasn't wearing anything sexy again. She just had on some shorts and a tee-shirt. "Hey Babydoll, what's going on?" Greg asked kinda groggy. "Sit down babe," She directed him, "your wife has made you breakfast." "My wife?" Greg chuckled, "Last night I was screwing a white girl and a Puerto Rican girl, and this morning I have a beautiful young black wife. This is amazing." "Look here mister," Priscilla explained, "while I'm your date, I'm playing the role of your loving loyal wife. All I ask for during the next week, is that you love me like you would your wife. This way I will know what real love is and I will never be deceived by these wanna be guys out here. Ok, deal?" "Ok, I can do that." Greg promised. He thought for a moment, "But if you are my wife, then you have to run my food business while I am at work." "I know," Priscilla said, "I'm way ahead of you. It's like you are just waking up." She dutifully served her man his breakfast just the way he liked it. Greg began realizing that Priscilla was more than a pretty face. She was really a sweet girl. He felt like he had to get her out of the strip club so she could have a good life. She deserved it.

Greg explained why his wings were so much better than other people's wings. "I slow bake them for one hour ten minutes before I leave the house. When someone orders some wings I pop them into the air fryer, which heats them back up and finishes the cooking process, the wings come out fall off the bone tender and very juicy. I then put whatever sauce the person wants onto the wings. Now you know my secret." Greg went to work thinking about Priscilla running his food truck. He got off from work and went to Tasha's house. He got the panties and went to where Priscilla was with his food truck. He put the panties into a plastic bag and put the plastic bag in a brown paper bag. When he arrived at the food truck, he gave Priscilla the panties. She looked at them closely and said: "These are 'Lise Charmel,' that's a very, very expensive brand of panty. I figure these panties cost $150. This tells me these are definitely Cynthia's panties without a doubt." "You are amazing."

Greg said, "Who could know something like that? So wife, how's it going?" "The wings are selling like hot cakes Greg!" She exclaimed with excitement, "This is the third time I've run out. So, what I did is called Angel who generally works at night. She came to help me run the truck. I left to get more wings and popped them in the oven following your recipe to the tee. I brought them back to the food truck and we sold out of them. I left again getting more wings which I popped in the oven and brought them back to sell, and we are almost out of them." "Babydoll, you did very well." Greg praised her, "Where's Angel?" "She had to get ready for work," Priscilla replied, "so she had to leave." "Did you pay her?" Greg asked. "I gave her $130. She was here from 10am-4pm," She detailed. "Was she ok with that?" Greg asked. "Yeah, she was happy with that." Priscilla reassured Greg. Priscilla and Greg stayed there and worked together selling wings like crazy until 10:30pm. After it was all said and done, Greg's business made 1,500 dollars profit for that day's work. Greg was pleased. "We need to get married Babydoll," Greg said, "you did so well today. You really helped me and taught me how I need to be able to resupply my wings as I go. This has to be a part of my business for it to be even more profitable. Priscilla, I could leave my job if I could make $1,500 dollars of profit every day." "I'm beat," Priscilla uttered exhausted, "I'm not going to be much good to you tonight baby." They both laughed. "I still got to pay you." Greg said. "I'm your wife. This is our business," Priscilla reminded him, "you and I made 1,500 dollars today. I'm paid." Once they got home, both of them collapsed on the couch in exhaustion.

Priscilla had been on her feet all day long. Greg took off Priscilla's shoes and put some warm water in a foot bath. He washed her feet. Then he dried them and started to massage her feet. "Oh my, that feels so good." She shared. Greg responded, "I got something for you. It's in the bag near you on the couch." She reached for the bag and pulled a card out. It was a thank you card Greg had picked up for her because she did such a good job with his good truck. The message he wrote was: "To the greatest wife a man could ever have. Today you out did yourself. I just want you to know that I greatly appreciate you and the work you have done to help me. Priscilla, I love you and I will always love you." Tears were welling up in her eyes. No one had ever thanked her for anything she had done in her life. Greg really appreciated what this young girl did for him and his business. Greg did all of this to give her a taste of what marriage was all about. He wanted her to know what true love was like. "Come here," She said, "give me a hug." Tears began to stream down her face as they embraced. Greg just held her in his arms until she dozed off. There was a knock on the door. Greg got up trying not to wake Priscilla. He opened the door. It was Nate his crazy friend. Nate walks in and heads to the refrigerator. "Hey man what's going on?" Nate said unaware Priscilla was in the room. "Nothing much, I'm good bruh." Greg answered. After checking the fridge, Nate realized someone else was in the room. He saw Priscilla starting to wake up. He paused. "Dude, what's up?" Nate asked referring to the beautiful young lady on the couch. "Hmmm, how do I explain?" Greg hesitated, "Ok, Tasha is out of town, and

Cynthia didn't want me to be alone. Cynthia sent Priscilla here to be my date until Tasha returns. Got it?" "WTF! Dude did you hear yourself?" Nate responded totally confused, "Did you understand the words that were coming out of your mouth? First of all, Tasha will kill you and secondly Cynthia, I don't get this threesome stuff. How does Cynthia take over your life from Tasha? Cynthia just basically reassigned you a temporary girlfriend. Where does she get this authority from?" "Let's just say Tasha doesn't know about Priscilla." Greg added. "And for both your sakes you better hope it stays that way." Nate replied, "Wait a minute. This is one of the naked hostesses. I totally recognize her now." "Hi Nate," Priscilla spoke half smiling, "good to see you." "Look Nate," Greg said, "what Tasha doesn't know can't hurt her. I'm not telling her. Priscilla is not telling her and you're not telling her. So, we are good." "Yeah…, except you left out Cynthia." Nate pointed out insightfully, "You are playing the most dangerous game, but you are the man. You are the man." Nate hung out for a little bit. Priscilla gave him some wings and something to drink. Then he took off.

Priscilla was a little concerned about the point Nate was making. Maybe Tasha will find out from Cynthia knowing how crazy she is. "Well, if that happens, we can say for sure that it will be the end of the threesome." Greg said, "That might actually be a good thing because this threesome business is killing me. Whatever you do Babydoll, don't worry. Just let everything take place like it is supposed to take place. Worrying about something is not going to change it." Greg put on some music and asked his lovely wife if she wanted to dance. The handsome couple slow danced to "So Amazing" by Luther Vandross. The simple things in life are often the best. Priscilla will never forget that song or that dance. It was truly special. At work the next day, Greg realized he and Priscilla had yet to have sex. She had been with him for a couple of days and they have done everything else but no sex. Their relationship was flowing. It was dynamic. They were getting along together very well. She was finishing his thoughts and he was surprising her with his warmth, support, and appreciation. Priscilla wasn't a stripper anymore to him. He was seeing another side of her. She was very smart and you could even say insightful. Priscilla didn't lie. Even if she was paid to lie, she didn't roll like that. She was loyal. She was royal. Priscilla had the attributes of a great person and a great wife. On top of all of this, she was the most beautiful girl at the club, and that's saying something. Priscilla was the envy of women everywhere. She had flawless young brown skin without a blemish, a perfect figure, full breasts, a perfectly shaped behind, beautiful eyes, and a wonderful personality. Greg got a little nervous because he realized that he was going to have to have sex with this precious gem at some point. How would he do it? He couldn't bang her like some call girl. No, it had to be real. It had to be special. That's what she deserves.

Meanwhile, Cynthia and Tasha had met a couple of girls downstairs in the casino gambling. They invited these girls up to their room because they had the male strippers coming up soon. The girl's names were Tammy and Lynn. They were childhood friends from Cincinnati, Ohio. They were two fun loving girls just taking a break from corporate America to blow off some steam. They loved to drink and party. "Hey don't fake us out now," Cynthia said, "the guys will be there at 11:00pm." "Are you kidding?" Lynn told them, "Wild horses couldn't keep us away. We are here to party baby." "We can split the cost with you," Tammy added, "money doesn't grow on trees ya know." "No, no, no!" Cynthia protested, "We got you this time. Our trip is all expenses paid. Come to the room at 10:45pm so we can set up and we can get our drink on." "We will be there." Lynn promised with excitement, "What to wear girlfriend?" "Not much and no bras." Cynthia said, "A party dress, a short skirt, something sexy, and simple. These stripper guys love to ask the women to get topless. Don't be scared ladies!" "Hey, we're big girls." Lynn responded, "Besides, what happens in Vegas stays in Vegas baby. It's time to let loose." They all laughed. Cynthia and Tasha had a lot of money left to spend so they decided to spend some on their new friends. They went to a very exclusive store ('if you have to ask you can't afford it' type of place) and purchased two very sexy dresses for Tammy and Lynn. One of the dresses was a sexy backless mini dress in metallic gold and the other dress was a deep V neck sexy mini mesh two-piece set in white also backless. The dip on the V-neck for the last dress came all the way down pass the belly button. These dresses were scandalously sexy and decadently expensive. Just perfect for this evening's event.

The girls arrived on time and were very happy to put on their new delectably sensuous dresses. They were true party girls ready to go. Cynthia whispered something to the girls after they were dressed while Tasha was in the other room. The girls took the pills Cynthia offered them and swallowed them down without hesitation. The strippers arrived on time. There were 4 of them. All of them were young, muscular, and handsome. There were two black guys, a white guy, and a hispanic guy. Several different flavors for the ladies' delight. Four ladies and four men. This was by design. Cynthia never stops planning. While the guys were setting up their music, Cynthia approached Tasha and offered her a pill. "Yeah girl," Cynthia said, "this will take you there. It will make you feel so good." "You know I don't do pills," Tasha replied, "I'm good. I will have a blast don't worry." "Ok, no problem." Cynthia responded as she popped the pill in her mouth right in front of Tasha, "This show is going to be off the chain girl. Did you see the muscles on that one guy?" "All of them girl. Each one of them has muscles." Tasha pointed out. Tasha was drinking Champagne. Little did Tasha know, Cynthia was not taking no for an answer. When Tasha was not looking, Cynthia poured the contents of one of the capsules into Tasha's drink. The strippers were dancing for the ladies in the living room area. Every time the stripper pulled off an item of clothing, the girls would scream. They all had dollar bills and were eagerly giving them to the strippers for encouragement. Cynthia loved to stuff the money down the tiny briefs the guys were wearing. She ran out of money and ran into the bedroom for more. "Girl," Tasha said, "where are you going?" "To get more money," Cynthia blurted out, half drunk. Tasha was curious where she was getting the money from so she followed her into the bedroom. Cynthia had a bag of money stashed away in one of the dresser drawers; the second one on the right. She was so drunk that she managed to spill the money from the bag onto the floor. "Holy shit," Tasha was astonished, "where did you get all of that cash money?" "It's the money we got to spend before we leave." Cynthia answered gathering up the cash and placing it back in the bag. Tasha thought, 'Why would Cynthia bring so much cash and she's a millionaire?' Tasha became very suspicious. "Where did this money come from Cynthia?" Tasha asked a little concerned, "Is this the money Jessica gave to the blackmailers?" "Maybe," Cynthia muttered drunk and under the influence of her own drugs. "I said maybe." "Oh my God! Did you blackmail Jessica Cynthia?" Tasha asked terrified of the possible answer. "Ummm…, maybe." Cynthia repeated again. "I don't believe this." Tasha uttered in panic, "You put this woman through hell, and now you and I are spending her money partying here in Vegas." "Oh, it's a harmless prank," Cynthia replied, "She is worth hundreds of millions. What is 50 thousand to her? It's nothing Tash. It's nothing." "Oh my God Cynthia," Tasha couldn't believe it, "you scared the shit out of this poor lady. Then you took her money. Jessica thought she would lose her husband behind this. Cynthia, you don't do things like this to people. It's wrong. You are going to give her the 50 thousand back. Period." "Tasha," Cynthia asked, "why do you have to be so strait-laced? Live a little. Enjoy yourself." "I will enjoy myself,"

Tasha declared, "right after you give me your word you will return the money to Jessica." "Awwwwwe, come on," Cynthia moaned, "do I have to?" "Yes, you have to," Tasha told her, "or I'm going home. I'm not spending this woman's money you stole from her. You have your own money. You are a millionaire Cynthia. You have no need to steal. And what's further, we don't have to spend like drunken sailors either to have fun. So if we need to cut back on the spending, I get it. But I need you to promise me you will fix this. You will give the money back to Jessica." "Ok, what do I tell her?" Cynthia asked. "Baby, I don't care what you tell her," Tasha answered, "just don't steal from your friends. Give her the money back and make this right. Promise me." "Ok, I promise," Cynthia muttered drunk, "I promise to give her the money back. All of it." "Thank you Cynt," Tasha replied relieved, "and please don't steal anymore." "Ok, let's get back to the party," Cynthia replied, "I got some money now!" She yelled as she ran back into the room with the strippers.

Priscilla was going to town with Greg's business. While he was at work, she was busy selling away. She really enjoyed the challenge and loved the fact they offered the customers a really good product at a reasonable price. It was good hard work for Priscilla, and it was very satisfying to her to hear well done every day when Greg got off from work. They were a great team and time was flying since they had been together. "You are the very, very, very best Babydoll," Greg said pleased, "I've got to reward you. You got any ideas?" "I just want more time with you," She admitted, "that's all." "Ok," Greg replied, "how does a 3-day weekend sound? Just you and I together. Where shall we go Babydoll?" "I have no clue," Priscilla said thoughtfully, "I never get vacations." "Ok, we are going to shut down this truck early, go home, and get on the internet. We will decide together." Greg announced. Priscilla was so happy. She was like a kid in a candy store, however, she was overwhelmed by the endless choices and possibilities. When they arrived at home, she went straight to the computer and started searching. "Let's not go away too far. I don't want to spend all our time driving." Greg cautioned. "Can we do a Bed & Breakfast?" Priscilla asked excited. "Absolutely." Greg answered. "I found a great one, but it's a little bit big for us." She said, "It's a 3-bedroom vacation house. It's not far at all. We can be there in less than an hour. What do you think babe?" "I'm there," Greg replied, "with all the work you did for our business, let's splurge. You're worth it and frankly, you've earned it. Call them and book it. Here's the card." She was on the phone the next minute. "It's on Boytoy," Priscilla said, "I love you so much. We are going to have so much fun. There are good restaurants nearby and we can still do entertainment in the city if we want cause we are not far. What am I gonna wear? This was unexpected. We can check in at 11am tomorrow. I need to go shopping babe. Can I put it on the card?" "Spoken like a real wife." Greg chuckled, "Put it on the card Babydoll. Put it on the card." Priscilla dashed out the door. She was headed to buy some clothes for the unexpected 3-day weekend.

Back at the luxury suite of Tasha and Cynthia in Vegas, things started to go into the absolute crazy phase. All the girls were in full party mode. There was no shame in their game at all. All four ladies were topless and drunk. Lynn was on her knees stroking the fully erect wood of one of the strippers. Tammy was in the bedroom making out with the hispanic stripper. Somehow her panties were already on the floor. Cynthia and Tasha were in the other room. Both of them wearing tiny red panties; the expensive kind. Tasha had the other two strippers under her control. For the first time in her life, she held the noticeably large dicks of two men in her hands at the same time. In her drunken stupor, she was stroking them up and down laughing and saying, "Who's your mamma? Who's your mamma young fellas?" Cynthia's perky titties were jiggling as she was laughing her head off having the time of her life. She loved seeing Tasha be a bad girl. The alcohol was flowing, titties were dancing, and these women were completely out of control. It was a good thing, for their sake, that these male strippers were young and strong.

Before the festivities began to spiral out of control, Cynthia had strategically placed 3 little cameras throughout the room Tasha and Cynthia were in. Her goal, of course, was to catch Tasha in a very compromising situation with these gorgeous young male strippers. She was making plans to break up Tasha and Greg. She wanted to keep Greg for herself. Needless to say, the video footage she was getting of Tasha stroking these two guys off at the same time was priceless. It was Cynthia's ammunition to destroy Tasha and Greg's relationship. The drug Cynthia placed in Tasha's drink earlier did two things. It made Tasha especially horny and it clouded her memory. When morning comes she would not remember any of the events from the previous night.

The next morning there were 4 topless women knocked out in the luxury suite. Cynthia woke up first and headed to the bathroom. Little by little the other ladies started to wake up. They all had headaches and they were all searching through the hotel room for their clothes. "Can't find my bra," Lynn whispered, "do you see it?" "You weren't wearing a bra," Tammy reminded her, "remember? 'No bras' was part of the dress code." "Right, of course." Lynn said. Tammy and Lynn gathered all their clothes putting them in a large shopping bag and headed back to their hotel room to get some much needed rest. They both had on dark shades. "Oh my goodness ladies," Tammy announced officially, "we had the best time ever. Just remember, 'What happens in Vegas stays in Vegas.' Contact us if you need help partying again. You know it's our duty to help you, and it was a pleasure also. Thanks for the sexy outfits. We will never forget last night. It was truly historic. Thanks, and good night, or good morning, or whatever." Tasha let them out, closed the door, and fell helplessly into bed pulling the covers over her head.

Meanwhile, on the way to the Bed & Breakfast, Priscilla shares her thoughts about Cynthia. "You know Greg," Priscilla revealed, "I've been doing a little research on Cynthia." "Really?" Greg asked, "Why?" "Because I care about you," She admitted, "and by extension I have to care about your girlfriend Tasha. I think Cynthia is more dangerous than you would think, or at least more dangerous than she appears." "How so?" Greg asked. "Ok," Priscilla answered, "I found out she has a degree in Psychiatry. That means she has knowledge of how different drugs affect a person's psychology. She could give you a drug to make you more aggressive sexually, she could give you a drug that could relax you thus putting you to sleep. She knows which drug would make you forget recent events. In other words, this woman can give you a drug so that she could control your behavior. Greg, that is too much power in the hands of someone who has no morals. I don't think Tasha is safe with her on this trip to Vegas." "So far everything Cynthia has done has not been that bad." Greg disclosed. "Yeah, maybe so," Priscilla replied, "but don't let your guard down. I'm focused on what she can do. Not what she has done." "But she would have to have a strong motive to do something really bad." Greg commented. "Is love a strong enough motive for you Greg?" She asked. "Hmmm, I didn't look at it like that," Greg acknowledged, "do you think Tasha is in danger?" "My personal opinion," Priscilla responded, "hell yes! I'm praying Tasha is even on the return flight with her. In my opinion, I don't put it pass her to completely eliminate the competition. I don't think it's probable, but I do think it's possible. It is hard to predict what Cynthia will actually do. So, don't take any chances with Cynthia." "Ok, so we know Cynthia will drug you without your permission," Greg pointed out, "because she did it to me so she will definitely do it to Tasha, if the need arises. Right?" "Right," Priscilla agreed, "Greg, maybe you should consider warning Tasha of this danger." "Yeah, I will call her," Greg replied concerned. "Another thing to consider," She said, "there is a conference of the Tru-max Corporation in Vegas this week and next week. All the big wigs will be there, including members of the board of directors. I find it quite a coincidence that Cynthia chose this time to be in Vegas." "I don't get what you're saying," Greg questioned somewhat confused, "what does Tru-max have to do with Cynthia?" "Tru-max is Cynthia's greatest competition," Priscilla explained, "her company competes directly with Tru-max for these super-lucrative government contracts. Greg there is a lot of money on the line. Not millions, but billions. Its dog eat dog out there. They are fighting for these contracts with their lives. It's brutal." "Ok, but what does that have to do with Tasha?" Greg asked a bit more concerned. "I don't know exactly," She responded feeling uneasy, "but Greg let me tell you this. At the club where I work, the rumor is that Cynthia uses the most expensive girls to serve or please the members of the board of her own company. These guys come in the club and they receive the best that we have to offer. We serve according to the wishes of the individual board member. I've talked to the girls that have slept with these guys. Often times, they are asked to do more than just sleep with them. They are asked to take pictures of documents in their brief case or even set up cameras recording the sexual act for bribery. Really dangerous stuff. Only a few of the girls had the nerve to do it, and trust me, Cynthia paid quite a high price for it. So, I say all this just to show you what this woman is capable of."

"I see what you're saying," Greg recognized. He was really paying attention to Priscilla. She has a street instinct, and the ability to figure out what is really going on before it goes down.

Chapter Eight
| <u>Tony</u> |

The girls finally got up and headed downstairs to get some much needed food. They were both still a little groggy, but functional. They figured after they got some nourishment in them, they will function much better, and feel better too. As they were eating, Cynthia started to explain the next activity they were going to do. It was presented to Tasha as a fun event like an adventure. "Tasha," Cynthia explained, "this is going to be something you have never done. We are going to this guy's room posing as call girls." "What!?" Tasha exclaimed, "Are you crazy? I'm not a call girl and you know Greg would kill me for having sex with another man." "Don't worry about Greg," Cynthia counselled her, "we are going to have some fun. He will never find out. No one can know because we will be wearing masks. No one will see our faces. We are going in pretending to be Mardi Gras party girls. It's the perfect cover." "Who is the dude?" Tasha asked. "Some big wig from a powerful technology company," Cynthia told her, "don't worry. No one is gonna know it's us. Live a little. You got to let loose now. You won't be able to do this after you get married girl. It's time for you to be wild and enjoy yourself. Greg is never going to find out. That's why we left him at home." "You are crazy Cynt," Tasha said as she got up to get some more food, "I'll be back." Cynthia put the contents of a capsule in Tasha's juice while she was away from the table. This drug would help Tasha let go of her inhibitions and do things that she normally wouldn't do. Tasha returned to the table, "Listen," Cynthia told her, "we got to buy some clothes so we can do this thing. There is a shop not far from here. So, after we finish eating, we will go buy some stripping attire." "Really?" Tasha asked. "Really," Cynthia replied, "have you ever stripped for anyone other than Greg? Girl let loose. Live a little we are in Vegas. We are in the promise land for fantasies. Do you think you could turn a man on with your body? Do you think you can make his nature rise by shaking your behind or showing him your tits? Have you ever wondered how beautiful you truly are to a total stranger? Tonight, you are going to find out exactly how sexy you are to other men and you're going to get paid handsomely for doing it. I guarantee you will get a healthy tip if you do a good job." "I don't know how to dance naked for a total stranger." Tasha admitted, "This is crazy." "Thank God Tasha I'm here." Cynthia reassured her, "I'm going to teach you and guide you, and we will go together and you will do well. You will become this dude's fantasy and he will enjoy the entire experience, and so will you. I promise. It will make you powerful." "Cynthia, I wasn't raised like this." Tasha pointed out. "No one will know." Cynthia replied, "Besides it's time for this old dog to learn some new tricks. Sometimes it's good to be bad."

The girls finished their breakfast and went shopping for sexy stripper outfits. "The colors are purple, gold, and green." Cynthia instructed, "I love the feathers, and don't forget the most important thing is the mask." "What am I wearing underneath this?" Tasha asked. "Here is a see thru mesh bra," Cynthia revealed, "let me find your size. Remember Tasha, you are dressing to undress." Once they were back in their luxury suite, the lessons on how to perform began. "Stripping is an art." Cynthia explained, "Forget what other people think of it. You must focus on your customer. He is the only person that matters. It's you and him. You have to connect sexually with him. You need to read him and make sure you have his attention. Figure out what turns him on. Either he wants to be dominated or he wants to dominate you. Someone has to be the boss." "How do you dominate a man?" Tasha asked. "Talk to him. Tell him what you want. Tell him what to do." Cynthia detailed, "It's pretty easy. You just have to have the courage to be in charge and don't take no for an answer. Get inside his head for real. You are the drug dealer. Your drug is sexual pleasure. He needs it. He's got to have it. He is a junkie. You are in control girl. Every time you get close to him touch him. Physical touch is powerful. Use it to your advantage. Maintain your confidence and your position of dominance. Don't let him try to take his control back. Tonight Tash, you are going to learn some things about yourself and your sexual personality. But most of all, have fun."

It was almost time for them to leave. Their client was at the Bellagio Hotel in a penthouse luxury suite. He was expecting one girl, but two showed up. The girls arrived in full Mardi Gras attire with masks. They knocked on the door and shortly thereafter, the door swung open. Let the games begin. "Hi, I'm Kassandra," Tasha greeted, "and this is Nicki." "Ladies welcome. My name is Tony," Now this took Tasha by surprise. She was looking at a handsome black man in his early thirties. She thought Cynthia told her he was some corporate big wig. Tasha expected a stereotypical white balding male in his fifties. Tony was hot. He didn't have any fat on his body. Obviously, he worked out. He was fine, intelligent, and polite. If it wasn't for Greg, she would be falling for this guy. Then it hit her. She was supposed to have sex with him. She is supposed to strip for this guy. She became nervous and she was intimidated. Tasha couldn't strip. She became self-conscious. She actually wanted to impress this guy.

The girls brought a hand-held speaker and needed to set up their music. As they walked to the bedroom, Cynthia told Tony, "Sir, we just need a brief moment to set up." "No problem ladies. Take your time." Tony responded. He stepped out of the bedroom to get himself a drink. "Girl, you didn't tell me this guy was fine." Tasha complained, "I'm scared. I can't take off my clothes in front of him. What if he doesn't like me? What if he doesn't respect strippers?" "OMG! What has happened to you?" Cynthia fired back, "Don't fall in love with the client. This is not a first date. He doesn't have to like you. Your job is to hypnotize this guy. He is a man. He has a dick. You can control him girl. Confidence – poise - power. Say it." "Confidence – poise - power." Tasha repeated it slowly. "You are up first Tash," Cynthia directed, "your job is to get this guy aroused. You were born to do this. You have the beauty, the body, the titties, and the ass. All you need now is the attitude, the confidence, and the power. Tonight, your fantasy to dance naked for a stranger will be fulfilled. Your dream of making hot passionate love to a total stranger will come true, and you will never see him again. I promise. I promise. You have nothing to lose. Get it together girl. You got this."

After that much needed pep talk, Tasha started to gain some confidence. She just needed to break the ice and get started, then she would be ok. The music started playing and Tasha began to relax. She started thinking, 'I got nothing to lose. I can seduce this guy. He is just a man. I don't care how rich and powerful he is. If he is so rich and powerful, how come he ain't got a girlfriend? I got this.' He walked into the bedroom and Tasha looked at him. "Tony, that is just what I need," Tasha (aka Kassandra) told him, "Do you mind if I have a drink?" "Kassandra, what is your pleasure?" Tony asked like a perfect gentleman. "Do you have any Champagne?" Tasha replied. "Absolutely Kassandra." Tony went to the bar to get her some Champagne, "So where are you from?" "No Tony," Tasha demanded, "the question is, where are you from? Kassandra is here to take care of your needs." Tony chuckled, "I'm currently living in North Carolina. Charlotte to be precise." "Hmmm, a southern boy." Tasha replied taking the glass of Champagne from his hand. She grabbed his hand and lead him back to the bedroom while taking a needed sip from the glass. "Right this way handsome." Tony smiled as he followed her to the bedroom. She had him sit on the bed and began rotating her hips slowly as she stared into his eyes.

Was he looking at her breasts? Was he fixated on her butt? What was his pleasure? She turned to Cynthia and had her come closer to whisper something to her. Cynthia went to change the music to Frankie Beverly and Maze "Southern Girl." The drug Cynthia had given Tasha was now in full effect now. Tasha was feeling it as her clothes fell away one piece at time. Tasha said to herself, 'Tony is definitely focused on my breasts. This is too easy.' Tasha was down to her panties when Cynthia went to the bed to sit next to Tony. She began rubbing her hand up and down his inner thigh getting closer and closer to his hardware. Her job was to get Tony undressed and get a condom on him. Tasha would do the rest after that. "I only requested one girl, how is it that I got two?" Tony asked. "There is no extra charge," Cynthia answered, "compliments of our company for our best and most loyal customers. Unless it bothers you of course." "No, it doesn't bother me at all." Tony replied quickly. "Gooood," Cynthia said, "let me top off your drink. Bourbon, right?" "Yes." "So how long you girls been with the agency?" Tony curiously asked, "I've never seen either of you." "I hope I'm pleasing to you?" Tasha inquired, "Would you prefer some other girls?" "No, no, no, I didn't mean it like that." Tony said recovering, "I find you girls excellent; even exquisite." "Tony you are a charmer, aren't you?" Tasha responded as she let her panties fall to the floor. Cynthia reentered the room with Tony's drink in her hand. She put a drug in his drink which should put him to sleep in about 30 mins. Cynthia handed him his drink and while he was sipping it, she managed to get a condom on him. Mission accomplished.

Cynthia vanished from the room as Tasha approached Tony

sitting on the bed. "Your soldier is standing at attention." Tasha acknowledged with a smile. "That is a good sign. You know what they say Tony, 'A hard man is good to find.'" She pushed him back further onto the bed and she straddled him cowgirl style. Allowing him to enter her body. Tony slowly reached for her mask. Tasha blocked him. "No, no, no, Mister," Tasha strongly affirmed, "This mask is part of the game we play, and I'm not finished playing with you yet." He smiled, "You are different than the other girls," Tony admitted, "you are not afraid of me." "Should I be Tony?" Tasha questioned. "Are you a bad guy?" "No, but I'm pretty rich." Tony expressed. "Ahhhh, let me tell you something Tony." Tasha responded, "You can buy sex, but you can't buy love." "Do you think I need love?" Tony asked. "What I think is irrelevant," Tasha answered, "but everyone needs love Tony; everyone." "Let me do something for you Tony," Tasha requested as she started to move her hips back and forth, working his joystick with extreme pleasure. She had one arm under her succulent breasts for support because they were rather large. Tony was fixated on them. Tony moaned, and Tasha remembered her training. She was in control and he was just a man. "Say my name Tony," Tasha coached him, "say my name." "Kassandra." Tony replied. Tasha leaned forward and whispered to him, "You honor me when you say my name Tony. A good woman loves to hear a good man say her name." "Am I a good man?" Tony asked. "Of course you are," Tasha affirmed, "you are the very best Tony. The very best. And Tony, I'm a good woman." "Yes, you are Kassandra." Tony said. Tasha rolled over and let Tony get on top of her for a bit.

Tony was inspired. It seems Tasha had his number. He was penetrating her at a very fast rate of speed. Normally Tasha would encourage him to slow up a little bit, but honestly, she was enjoying it. Tasha wondered, 'Where is Cynthia?' Tasha noticed her conscience was not bothering her about having sex with this man. She listened to Cynthia and half believed what Cynthia taught her. Tasha just viewed it as having fun and exploring her sexuality. Tony pulled Tasha to the edge of the bed and he spread her legs. As he thrusted himself inside of her, she felt extreme pleasure. She thought to herself, 'Just let this guy enjoy it.' With each thrust her breasts jumped, and she noticed Tony was looking at her breast as he continued to penetrate her. She laughed to herself because Tony was getting himself off on bouncing her titties. He was just a man, and Tasha was his toy his plaything. This turned out to be easier than Tasha had expected.

Cynthia entered the room naked and was trying to get the attention off of Tasha. She interrupting them and maneuvered Tony away from Tasha so that he was lying on his back. Cynthia pulled the condom off and replaced it with another. She was clearly taking over. She started with her traditional blowjob of course. She followed the blowjob with the cowgirl position, working him slowly, and deliberately. "Ohhhh, Nicki," Tony released, "Ohhhh, Nicki." She continued, but started speeding up a bit. Instead of going back and forth, she started going round and round. Cynthia was going to bring this guy to a climax. Tasha could not understand why. They were supposed to be there for 2 hours. You don't climax the guy the first 30 mins. Tony exploded into the condom. After his orgasm he went limp for a bit. Cynthia laid there with him for a few minutes. Tony dozed off quite quickly falling asleep. Cynthia pulled herself from the bed slowly as not to wake Tony. "Get your stuff girl," Cynthia told her, "let's get out of here." "What?" Tasha asked feeling confused, "Aren't we supposed to be here for 2 hours?" "I got what I came for," Cynthia replied, "and you got your fantasy. By the way girl, I'm proud of you. You came through like a trooper. Tasha, you did an outstanding job. This guy will ask for us again. I guarantee it." The girls put on their clothes and got out of there. Tony was still fast asleep.

Priscilla and Greg arrived at the Bed & Breakfast. They unloaded the car and got settled in. The place was amazing. It was spacious, clean, well-stocked, and in a wonderful location. They were pleased with their choice. They were hungry so they went to a nice local restaurant for a great meal. "You know that today is Friday," Priscilla asked innocently, "and you know what that means right?" "I don't know what you're getting at." Greg answered. "Cynthia told me your threesome gets together on Fridays to do their thing." Priscilla explained, "Since I am replacing Cynthia and Tasha, I am obligated to continue this practice. In fact, I have to replace two women for you. Normally you would get two women on Friday, right?" "Ahhhh, right," Greg responded, "but you don't have to. . ." "I have to play my part Greg," Priscilla insisted, "You don't think I can be as good as two women in bed Greg?" "You know I didn't say that." Greg said smiling. "For whatever reason Greg, we have not had sex since I've been assigned to you." Priscilla pointed out the obvious, "Maybe I've put on some pounds and my hubby doesn't find me attractive anymore. Or maybe we have been working so hard that we have both been exhausted at the end of the day. Or maybe we have been so busy bonding and having fun that we just forgot to make love. Or maybe you are afraid to make love to me because I'm not a booty call anymore, and there are serious feelings and emotions here. You know I only have one week to be in your life then I am gone forever. Whatever the case may be, the time is up. Tonight you get a double dose of me. I hope you're ready big guy. I know I am." She stared at him as a very subtle self-confident smile creeped on to her face. Greg was speechless. They finished their meal and decided to catch a movie while they were out.

Greg promised to spend some time with Priscilla and that's exactly what he was going to do. Whatever she wanted to see, or do, he was down for it. Greg was a little nervous when they finally returned to the vacation house. He really didn't know how to make love to Priscilla. Her status changed in his life and he was stuck. He couldn't fuck her. She was his companion and wasn't a call girl to him anymore. If he made real love to her this would be a disaster. He could actually fall out of love with Tasha and in love with Priscilla. And no matter what he decided to do, Priscilla would know. She could read him and read the entire situation. Greg didn't have a game plan for making love to Priscilla.

Once they returned to their B&B room, Priscilla talked with Greg. "Babe, I want to show you some outfits I picked up," Priscilla said, "and I want you to be completely honest with me. Tell me which ones you like the best and why. Don't lie homeboy because I will know. And I will get you." "And you will get me?" Greg asked laughing, "I'm afraid, I'm very afraid." "Get comfortable." She charged him as she was closing the curtains so no one could look in on them. The first outfit was a very short skirt. It was extremely short being 3 or 4 inches in length. It was fuchsia in color and very shiny. It couldn't cover her entire booty. The cheeks of her full booty were hanging out which Greg found sexy being the man that he is. She was wearing fuchsia pasties in the shape of hearts to cover her nipples. "My, my, my, my, my," Greg said completely captivated, "that is scandalous babydoll." "You like it?" she asked. "Hell yeah!" Greg exclaimed with excitement. "I like the color. It's you. I like the way it makes your butt look and this outfit gives me an unobstructed view of the natural curves of your body which are magnificent." "Really baby?" Priscilla said smiling, "I'm glad you like it. Ok, I'll be right back." The next outfit was equally scandalous. Priscilla had on black crotchless panties with the coochie in full view. She had on a push-up bra with the nipples pulled up out of the bra on full display. She walked over to her man and stood right in front of him. Greg's eyes were focused intently on her chacha. The tender wrinkled lips of her pussy mesmerized Greg. He was lost in time staring at it. She didn't rush him at all. Priscilla just stood there and let him take it in. In a soft voice she asks, "Babe, what do you think of this outfit?" She already knew what he thought. She could read it on his face. "Oh my, girl," Greg replied slowly like he was waking from a deep sleep, "this is lovely. I like it. Ahhhm, it reveals your natural. . . I mean it shows off your. . . It's hard to explain." "Babe, this is very easy," She commented, "just tell me why you like this outfit." "Uhhhm, yeah," Greg explained, "it is beautiful, and black looks good on you. I like it because nothing is hidden. Your natural beauty is on display." "Ok, be right back." Priscilla said running off. The third outfit wasn't really an outfit per se. Priscilla had on black fishnet stockings that came to the middle of her juicy thighs. She wore black high heel pumps. She had on fuchsia lip stick and earrings. Her nipples were covered with a dab of whipped cream and her pussy was covered with a line of whipped cream.

This young 24-year-old girl was viciously beautiful and there was no denying it. Her figure was perfect. Her skin was perfect. She was flawless. Few men get to enjoy beauty at this level. Greg felt like he was the luckiest man on the planet. There were going to be no more outfits this evening, Greg had seen enough. He reached out and took her by the hand leading her to the bedroom. "Wait baby, I have other outfits. I'm not finished yet." Priscilla disclosed. "Oh Babydoll, you are finished. Trust me." Greg remarked smoothly. Priscilla smiled at Greg. Her plan to arouse him worked, and much faster than she thought. Greg licked the whipped cream off her nipples. He loved it. He sucked her nipples while holding her breasts in his hands softly. He took his time. Then

Greg got on his knees to lick the whipped cream off of her essence. He spent some quality time down there for her personal stimulation. She loved it so much she couldn't hold back from moaning softly. Priscilla had to break through to Greg, much like Cynthia had to break through to get Greg to let go and love her passionately. Priscilla was brilliant at reading Greg and connecting with him. Greg had finally let go. He wanted to love Priscilla with all his heart and all his might. He wanted her to feel what true love felt like. That Friday night, the emotion between Greg and Priscilla was fiery, passionate, and true. Priscilla was unable to distinguish between love and sex, it was the same thing. Normally she could separate love and sex. It was her job as a call girl to be able to do that or she couldn't function at her business. Still, this night was different. She loved Greg and he was making love to her. She too had to let go so she could become one with Greg. Greg rolled her on the bed. With Priscilla on her back and her legs slightly opened, he began penetrating her deeply. He maintained a steady pace, but not too fast. He checked with her to make sure it felt good. She let him know she was on cloud nine. After some time, Greg put her ankles on his shoulders. Priscilla opened her mouth in surprise and smiled in anticipation. She knew exactly what Greg was about to do to her. He was going to try to find the right angle to penetrate her inside and stimulate the outside of her pussy at the same time. He tried continuously to find the correct angle of penetration. Finally, he heard her response. He kept going and the pleasure in Priscilla kept building greatly until she climaxed. Her entire body trembled and she clung to Greg. She held him with all her might. At that moment Greg became her man. Priscilla had to rest for a moment after such a powerful climax. When she thought about it, that was the first time a man gave her an orgasm. Greg held her in his arms and said, "I love you Babydoll." She felt safe and secure with him. After resting for a while, Priscilla was ready to satisfy her lover. She got on top of Greg and begin to work those hips. She was talking to him while she was doing it. "Babe, that was the most wonderful thing that anyone has ever done to me; for me," Priscilla admitted, "I will never forget it and I will forever be in your debt. Now let me return the favor." Greg was trying to be as strong as he could as she worked her young hips vigorously, round and round in the cowgirl position. Priscilla had her full weight resting on his manhood. There was no way any man could hold up to that kind of intense sexual stimulation over an extended period of time. He hung in there as long as he could, but she made him explode in pleasure. He turned her on her side so he could pull out quickly. She laughed because she knew exactly what she was doing. They shared a night of passionate love and Priscilla was the equal of two women that night. She wore Greg out.

"Damn!" Cynthia shouted while she was on the phone, "I knew something was missing. It must have been in the safe. Ok then, I will have to go back. I will call you back later. Good bye." "What was that all about?" Tasha asked. "I messed up Tash," Cynthia confessed, "when we were with Tony there was one set of documents that I didn't get pictures of. You remember when I disappeared for a stretch of time while you made love to Tony? Right? Well I was on a mission from my company to copy some papers from his briefcase in the living room. I got pics of everything I needed except one thing. I didn't get pics of the documents that described the prototype of the hand-held control panel. It is like an I-pad that controls an entire plane. It is what I went over there to get in the first place. Girl, we have got to go back, but this time without the masks." "Why no masks?" Tasha asked. "Because they have technology that can detect me opening that briefcase." Cynthia explained, "They may be looking for Kassandra and Nicki, but they are not looking for Tasha and Cynthia." "Oh my goodness," Tasha said, "I could go down for breaking and entering." "No Tash," Cynthia replied, "we didn't steal anything. All his papers are still there inside his briefcase. We are clean. They could even search our room and would find nothing." "So, what's the plan?" Tasha asked a little scared. "Girlfriend, I need you to seduce Tony," Cynthia said, "and see if you could get both of us invited back up to his room. He has seen me before so I will have to wear some dark glasses and a baseball cap to help me conceal my face from him. You sexy up to him really good and make him want it bad. When he invites you up to his room, you insist that your girlfriend go also for safety. After all, you don't really know him." "I will teach you how to get a man to take you back to his room." Cynthia continued, "You are not Tasha. I will give you another name. He is a known quantity to you, right? You know he is attracted to your breasts, so you will dress appropriately to attract him. You are not a stripper. You must change your approach. We need to get you some super expensive clothes that only he would recognize. You are a successful business woman who doesn't need a man for money or security. You play hard to get, yet you leave a trail of bread crumbs for him to want you. Don't chase him. Ignore him, but make him see you and feel you. Let him convince you to trust him. Once he decides that he wants to pursue you, look him up and down like you are considering it. Then you can ask him some questions. Questions that indicate to him you are considering sleeping with him." "Once you accept his invitation to go up to his room," Cynthia went on to say, "toy with him. Make it look like you are having second thoughts. He will have to work harder to get you up to his room. Ok, once in his room, you are not a stripper. You are not a call girl. You don't make any moves. Let him use his game to seduce you. He has to undress you and get you to the bed. No doubt he will use alcohol. He may even offer you some pills; who knows. While you are making out with Tony in the bedroom, I will open the safe and get pics of the documents I'm looking for. Once that is done, I will interrupt your love making and tell you that I have an emergency, and I have to go. So, you have to go. Get his number, apologize, and promise him you will get back together with him and next time it will be better." Cynthia went on to explain a lot to Tasha about the psychology of seducing a rich man. Nonetheless, she knew there was already a connection between Tony and Tasha. They were on the same wave length. Tasha definitely had the advantage since Tony doesn't know that it is

Kassandra he will be dealing with. This plan had a real chance of working. Tasha and Cynthia went shopping for the dress that would hook Tony. Poor guy doesn't have a chance. The dress they selected was stunning. It was purple with a fuchsia belt around the waist. It had a deep V neck that went all the way to Tasha's belly button. Needless to say, you couldn't wear a bra with this dress. Half her breasts were on display at all times and every time she moved to the right or left, the breasts swayed drawing unlimited attention. The bottom part of the dress was a tight skirt which highlighted the fullness of her booty. The dress was tasteful, but it was also scandalous. If she leaned forward in this dress, you could see her full naked breasts. This dress magically made Tasha deliciously irresistible eye candy to Tony. "Now we just have to find Tony," Cynthia said.

The girls headed to the Bellagio hotel knowing Tony could have been anywhere in Vegas. However, if you have a luxury penthouse suite at the Bellagio, maybe you are going to use their facilities first. The girls split up to see if they could find Tony. That night they had no luck. Tony didn't show up. Every night they would come to the Bellagio hoping to find Tony, but it didn't happen. Sunday night, Monday night, and Tuesday night, they still did not see him. Tasha carried the sexy purple dress in a bag everyday she went to the Bellagio, just in case they would see him. According to Cynthia's sources, he was still staying at the Bellagio and would be there until Friday. On Wednesday, the girls did their shopping inside at the Bellagio. They kept their eyes open for him. Cynthia was dressed in a baseball shirt and a baseball cap with dark glasses. She made it impossible to recognize her face. After searching through all the slot machines, Tasha saw him sitting at the bar. He was scoping out the women in the casino. Tasha ran and found Cynthia. "Go in the bathroom and put the dress on quickly," Cynthia demanded, "I will keep my eye on him." When Tasha returned he was still at the bar. "Ok, you know the plan, right?" Cynthia asked. "Right." Tasha answered.

They walked over by the bar to make sure Tony got a real good look at Tasha and her titties. "I'm going to walk by him," Tasha indicated, "I want to touch him and make him feel me." "Ok. Remember everything we talked about," Cynthia reminded her, "you are not a stripper. Make him want you. Make him chase you. Ignore him, yet bait him. He's fishing for you when you are the real hunter here. He is the one in danger and doesn't realize it." "Yeah, I got it." Tasha articulated in deep concentration as she headed to the bar. She bumped his bar stool pretty hard, and pretended to almost fall down. He jumped up and helped steady her by grabbing her firmly. "I'm so sorry," she said, "sometimes I can be so clumsy. I didn't spill your drink, did I?" She put her hand on his shoulder touching him. Tony was standing over her looking down the deep V neck of her beautiful dress as she was slightly bent over brushing herself off. Her breasts were completely exposed to his view, and they swayed a little as she steadied herself. Tony had a hard time pulling his eyes away from that titillating view. He received a full view of those irresistibly delicious titties. Tasha noticed that he took the bait. "No, no, no, are you ok?" Tony examined. "I'm good. I'm good now." Tasha answered, "Thank you. You are so kind." She turned and walked away. She was headed back to the table where Cynthia was sitting. Tony tracked her down and tapped her on the shoulder. As she turned around he asked, "Hey, can I get you a drink?" "I'm here with my friend," Tasha confessed innocently, "It wouldn't be right for me to leave her alone." "No, no. It's no problem." Tony reassured her, "How 'bout I get both of you some drinks and if you don't mind the company, I could join you at your table so we don't leave your friend alone." "I don't know you sir," Tasha replied, "can I even trust you?" Tony laughed, "My bad," He reacted, "allow me to introduce myself. I'm Tony. A very good guy that you can trust." "Hmmm ok. I'm Tangela," Tasha responded, "but everyone just calls me Tangie." "I'm honored to meet you Tangela," Tony replied with a smile. Tony went to the table with Tasha (aka Tangela). "What would you ladies like to drink?" Tony asked politely. "Rum and coke," Cynthia answered. "I'll take an orange daiquiri." Tasha added. "I'll be right back." Tony answered. "When he gets back, I'm going to go to the ladies' room." Cynthia explained. "I can't risk him seeing my face. Did he see your titties?" "Yes, he got a good long look." Tasha stated, "You're right, sometimes it is good to be bad." "Good, you are on track." Cynthia conveyed, "You know Tash, you are getting really good at this. Now all you got to do is get Tony to invite you up to his room. Remember everything we talked about." Tony came back to the table and Cynthia took a sip of her drink and excused herself. She headed to the ladies' room. "Tangela has anyone ever told you that you have the most beautiful light brown eyes?" Tony asked. "You're a charmer aren't you?" Tasha responded. "What do you do?" Tony asked. "I own a small book publishing company." Tasha explained, "We print a wide variety of different kinds of books." "What about yourself?" Tasha asked. "Well, I own a tech company that works primarily with the government." Tony answered, "We manufacture devices used to help diagnose and analyze the workings of fighter jets." "You are making the big, big bucks then," Tasha suggested, "I get lost on all that technical stuff though. I'm sure it's very interesting." The two of them sat there talking it up for another 45 mins or so. Tony was very attracted to Tasha and Tasha was working her magic to get him to ask her up to his room. "I have an idea," Tony said, "why don't you and your friend join me in my penthouse suite for dinner tonight?" "Hmmm, I don't know Tony." Tasha replied playing the game, "First of all, we don't know you. Secondly, we don't want to intrude on your life or your privacy. Thirdly, what would your wife or significant other think?" "Tangela, you never cease to amaze me." Tony responded, "Now you know good and well I don't have a wife or a significant other." "What!? A charming, handsome, rich man like you still on the market?" Tasha questioned him, "Come on Tony. I wasn't born yesterday." "Do you see a ring?" Tony objected, "I once had a girlfriend and it didn't work out, that's all. That's pretty normal. All relationships don't work out. I'm sure you've had your share of bad ones too." "I'm not saying that I will do dinner with you," Tasha speculated, "but if we did have dinner in your penthouse suite, what would we do? Order McDonalds, Kentucky Fried?" "Tangela you slay me." Tony chuckled, "Only the best for my new friends. It's my chance to finally impress you. I'm pulling out all the stops. You tell me what you want and I will have the finest chefs in Vegas prepare it for you. From drinks to the appetizers - to the main course - to the succulent desserts. I promise you the best meal you have ever seen Tangela." "Umm huh," Tasha responded in a doubting tone, "You are a pretty fancy guy, huh?" "Please be my guest," Tony asked graciously, "you will not regret it." "Ok," Tasha replied, "everything depends on what my girlfriend says." "Fair enough." Tony agreed. Cynthia quickly approved the idea. "Ladies, give me one hour and meet me in my suite." Tony pronounced as he whipped out his cell phone. "Hey write down your room number before you leave." Tasha reminded him. Tony handed Tasha his number smiling at her as he walked off. After he was gone, Cynthia celebrated Tasha, "Well played young lady. You had that guy eating out of the palm of your hand. Tangela, you get him in that bedroom for 10-15 mins and that is all I need."

Greg and Priscilla were really settling in and enjoying their 3-day weekend. The chef from the Bed & Breakfast would come by at 10:30am to cook breakfast for them. The chef was a very nice older lady named Sophia who could really cook. This of course was of interest to Greg. He was always learning new cooking techniques to add to his repertoire. "I'm doing an apple crumble for you guys." Sophia said, "If you love apples, you're gonna love it. If you love apple pie, you're gonna love it." "Then we are going to love it." Greg replied. "But why are you making the dessert first?" "Because there is a 45 min wait time to allow this dish to cool and to set up nicely." Sophia explained, "You can't rush the cooling down time. I must get this dish started first." Breakfast was wonderful. Priscilla just loved this homey feeling of being there with Greg and doing whatever they wanted to do. They planned their day together to just be relaxed and let life flow to them. Sophia addressed them, "It's time. The crumble is ready." Like two kids scrambling down the hall for dessert, Greg and Priscilla came running to the table. Sophia scooped it out onto their plates. It was warm with the intense smell of cinnamon and butter. "Who wants vanilla ice-cream?" Sophia questioned. "Do you really have to ask that question?" Greg asked. "Hook a sista up Sophia." Priscilla said playfully, "Hook me up! Don't be stingy." They laughed and had a great time. The simple pleasures in life are the best.

Sunday was their last day together at the vacation house and honestly, they spent most of it in bed playing with each other. Greg oiled and massaged Priscilla's whole body. Priscilla took care of Greg's special tool. They had sex and made love all morning and deep into the afternoon. It was pleasant and relaxing. Very memorable. They packed up the car and returned to Greg's place at the end of their wonderful 3-day weekend vacation. Monday came and Greg went to work. Priscilla operated the food truck like a pro. Angel showed up and helped Priscilla. When Greg got off from work, he helped Priscilla. They had that side business going and the popularity of it was growing too with Priscilla doing the business during the day. Only Greg didn't let the business operate too late. He shut everything down around 7pm to have some time to spend with Priscilla. He didn't want to wear her out with all of these long days. Money wasn't the most important thing. When they got home, Greg told her, "I want to take you out to a very nice restaurant." "Really?" Priscilla asked genuinely surprised, "Where are we going?" "It's a down home restaurant that serves typical southern food with a sophisticated flare." Greg described, "They have taken our traditionally southern dishes and made them fancy. Everyone who has gone there tells me it is off the chain, and you get good portions. I get some really good ideas I can add to my way of cooking the same thing." "Oh my Greg!" She said with excitement, "That sounds soooo good." They dressed up together nicely. Greg put on a suit jacket and Priscilla put on a stunning fuchsia dress. She was strikingly beautiful and very radiant in that dress. They were a handsome couple who would catch your eye if you were in that restaurant. Once they were seated, Greg could not wait any longer. He had a gift for Priscilla which was burning a hole in his pocket. "I have something for you Babydoll," Greg expressed, "I hope you like it." Greg showed her a box. A long rectangular box. He opened it right in front of her. Priscilla's eyes lit up and were fixed on it. It was like her brain was trying to make out what it was. She stared at it, and finally raised her eyes to Greg in his handsome suit. It was a beautiful gold necklace with a heart on it. It had a single diamond in the center of the heart. "Ohhhhh," was all Priscilla could say. Not only was she surprised, but she was thinking about what this meant for their relationship. "Ohhhhh Greg," Priscilla sounded, "it's so precious. What does it mean?" "It's a sign between you and me Priscilla." Greg replied, "It's a sign of true love." "Awwwwe," She uttered as she got up to hug her man with tears in her eyes. They both stood up to hug at the exact moment the server, a young girl, arrived at their table. They kinda bumped her as Priscilla threw her arms around her superman. "Sorry." Greg begged the waitress' pardon. "Wow," replied the waitress, "are we celebrating something special here?" "Yes," Priscilla answered breathlessly with tears streaming down her face, "yes, we are celebrating true love. Look what he gave me." "Oh my God," the waitress said, "I love it. It's so gorgeous. It's dazzling. Let me help you put it on. Oh, it goes so well with this dress which is also gorgeous. I think it's your night girl. I'm so jealous." They all laughed and were seated. After they ordered Priscilla says, "Baby, I'm going to the Ladie's Room. I want to see how this thing looks like on me." "Wait Babydoll," Greg urged her, "let me take a picture first." One of the dining guests from a nearby table proposed, "Let me take a picture of the both of you for this momentous occasion." "Thanks," Greg told him, "you are the man." He snapped a couple of perfect pictures. "Thanks again." Greg said sincerely. Priscilla ran off to the bathroom.

The girls, Tasha and Cynthia, went up to the penthouse suite exactly one hour later as instructed by Tony. Tony opened the door and there was a feast laid out before them. The barbecue was fall off the bone tender. There was filet mignon, fish, turkey, and beef. The ladies were offered drinks. Cynthia chose a peach margarita and Tasha chose her favorite, Champagne. They were seated in the dining room and dinner was served. Tony was a gracious and wonderful host. The wait staff was professional and helpful. They explained everything and stayed out of the way. Cynthia had a strawberry milkshake for dessert, and Tasha had an ice cream sundae with nuts, bananas, whipped cream, strawberry sauce, chocolate sauce, and cherries. The meal was 'to die for.' Even Tasha had to give it to the host for an incredible meal, and an incredible experience. The staff cleaned up and left very quickly. It was time for Tony to make his move. "Tangela," Tony said, "I'm glad you enjoyed the meal. I would like to show you the view from this luxury penthouse suite. It is amazing." He walked her into his bedroom and took her over to the curtains in the far corner of the room. He instructed her, "Stand right there." Tony walked over to the wall and hit a button. The curtains started to slide to the left revealing a beautiful view of the strip and other hotels near them. If you looked down you could see the water show at the base of the Bellagio. The view was live. It was spectacular. It was breathtaking.

Tasha became Tangela. She was so impressed with this attractive black corporate leader. "Oh my God that's incredible!" Tasha exclaimed, "Your view is unbelievable Tony!" Tasha became a little weak and forgot he was supposed to be chasing her. She walked over to him putting her arms around him giving him a long passionate kiss. Then she snapped out of it saying, "Oh, I'm sorry.

I didn't mean to be forward like that." "Baby, it's ok." Tony assured, "Let's get those shoes off so you can be comfortable." He sat her down and kneeled before her taking off her shoes. He began to massage her feet. "Oh my goodness," Tasha released, "that feels so good. I've been on my feet all day." "I studied to be a Massage Therapist," Tony informed, "I like to think that I'm very good. Let me give you a massage." "Tony, are you going to be a bad boy?" Tasha joked. "Not at all my lady." Tony answered, "I will be a perfect gentleman." "Sometimes it's good to be bad Tony," Tasha told him playfully. "Here, put on this robe." Tony encouraged her handing her a beautiful expensive silk robe. "And you want me to take off my dress?" Tasha asked, "You're smooth. A girl will get sweep right off her feet if she is not careful." "No worries." Tony declared, "Just go into the bathroom, take off the dress, and put on the robe." I will check on your friend."

Tony walked back to the dining room and saw Cynthia still drinking her milkshake. "If you don't mind waiting for a few minutes, I promised Tangela a massage," Tony explained, "I will be done shortly. You can wait in the living room. If you want you can get on the computer, or watch TV. I promise I will not be long. Tony went back into the bedroom and pulled a massage table from the closet. He set it up and put towels over it to make it more comfortable for Tangela (Tasha). He got some massage oils from the closet as well. Tasha came out of the bathroom and walked right pass Tony while maintaining extreme eye contact. She whispered, "Don't you try anything… rich boy. I'm watching you." Tony laughed. With her back to Tony, Tasha dropped her robe to the floor. She was wearing nothing but white panties. Very tiny expensive panties. They barely covered her very shapely behind which Tony was studying intently. Tasha paused for the full effect of her glorious body to sink into Tony's mind. She knew he was memorizing every curve. Then a thought hit her that made her panic. Maybe this guy will remember her naked body from the previous night. She quickly jumped on the massage table face down. She started to get really nervous. 'Please don't let this guy remember my naked body from yesterday.' Tasha prayed to herself.

Like a gentleman, Tony took a white towel and covered Tasha's behind. Then he warmed up the oil by rubbing it in his hands for a few seconds. His hands felt good on Tasha's back. He was truly relieving her stress. She began to relax and let go. "How's that Tangela?" Tony inquired, "Am I doing it too hard? How does it feel?" "Mmmmm," Tasha answered, "it's great. You have a really good touch." "Is that you Tangela?" Tony asked, "You gave me a compliment. 'Where is Tangela and what have you done with her?'" Tony joked. "I know I have been hard on you." Tasha sighed, "You know I can't leave myself vulnerable to a total stranger, and I can't come across as an easy target. I have to play hard to get." "Wow, bare naked honesty." Tony replied, "What have you done with Tangela?" "Tangela is right here Tony." Tasha affirmed, "Ohhhh, that feels good." Tony was massaging the base of her spine. He was dangerously close to her booty. Now Tasha wanted him to go for it. She wanted to feel his strong hands massaging her behind.

Tony was playing it smart. He would be a gentleman the first night to win her trust. Tasha had to be careful here. This is the type man she could actually fall for. To make matters worse, she already had sex with this guy and really enjoyed it. Tony started massaging her legs. He skipped over her behind and went to her legs. Well, massaging her legs was getting Tasha aroused. The closer he got to the top of her legs, the closer he got to her coochie. This was driving Tasha crazy. She was no longer in control. She had to hang on until he was finished. This should have given Cynthia enough time to do what she needed to do and then they could leave.

Tasha thought to herself, 'Don't forget the plan. Stick to the plan.' After a bit more massaging by Tony, she changed and thought to herself, 'To hell with this plan. I only live once.' "I hope you are not going to give me a partial massage and leave my behind out." Tasha advised Tony, "You have permission to remove my panties if they are in your way." Tony's nature began to rise. Now he had to be careful. However, he wanted to play along with Tasha like he was a professional and this wouldn't bother him at all. "As you wish my lady." Tony moved quickly. He slid the towel up to cover her back, and he slid the panties down her legs removing them completely in a single stroke like a pro; done like a true expert. "You've done this before." Tasha stated completely relaxed. Tony oiled up his hands again and started massaging her behind. His strong hands rubbing on her booty was more than any woman could take. Yet, Tasha remained cool the best she could. She was getting wet and even worse still, she wanted him to do her right there.

Certainly 10-15 mins had gone by; where was Cynthia? What was taking her so long? This was hard work and Tasha didn't know how much longer she could resist this guy. Tony continued working her luscious behind. He was starting to lose it too. Both of these new friends were about to explode. Tasha was Tony's kind of woman. A strong woman that would stand up to him, but at the same time, could be honest with him, and could share with him. He wanted someone that was his equal. Tasha displayed that she wasn't scared of him, but Tasha finally reached the point of no return. She jumped up off that massage table grabbing Tony's hand leading him to the bed. This was 'what happens in Vegas stays in Vegas part 2.' She didn't say a word. She pulled his clothes off and pushed him back onto the bed! The hungry couple went at it like a pair of horny teenagers! Tony lost it at the same time Tasha lost it! Tasha was on her back and Tony was penetrating her passionately. Then Tasha got on the top and started working it pleasing her new friend. Both of them crossed the line. Tasha was falling for this guy and she was planning to come over here to his penthouse suite tomorrow for part 3. She completely forgot about Greg. And as for Tony, he doesn't let women get to him like this. He is a pro at simply fucking a girl and moving on. This is not that. He finally found someone he could connect with and someone he could trust, Tony loved Tasha's brutal honesty. The two were going at it like crazy when Cynthia entered the room. "Oh, I'm sorry," Cynthia said apologetically, "so sorry to interrupt, but I got an emergency. My kid fell out of a tree. They are taking him to the hospital. Tangela, I got to go." Tasha rolled out of the bed genuinely embarrassed, "I'm so sorry Tony," She apologized, "but I got to go help my friend." Tasha ran into the bathroom. She put her dress back on and was leaving the room when Tony grabbed her and kissed her deeply. "I'll come back tomorrow." Tasha promised in a whisper, "I'll be back and we will finish what we started baby." "I need you girl." Tony proclaimed to her, "I can't live without you." They kissed again and Tasha ran out with her friend. In the rush she left her expensive white panties on the massage table. Something for Tony to remember her by perhaps.

The two girls ran down the hall and got on the elevator. Cynthia was trying to send the photos via her cell phone. "I can't get a signal. Stop the elevator at the next floor." The girls got off the elevator and Cynthia ran to a window down the hall. "Ok, I got a signal," She sent the pics off. She quickly found an open-air balcony and tossed her phone over the balcony. It shattered into a thousand pieces near the back entrance of the hotel. The girls calmly reboarded the elevator and went to the first floor. They were headed to the door when hotel security stopped them. "Ladies, come with us." The guard told them. "Why!?" Cynthia announced. "We've done nothing wrong." "We are going to have to put you under arrest. There was a break-in in one of our penthouse suites. We have the two of you on camera exiting the room just a few minutes ago. Wait here. The police will arrive in about 1 minute." Cynthia called Paradise with Tasha's phone. "Rose, I need you on the next flight to Las Vegas." Cynthia commanded, "They are arresting me and Tasha for breaking into a safe. Nothing was taken. My phone fell off a balcony and shattered. Get me out of jail. Bring some money." Rose understood. She knew Cynthia probably opened the safe taking pictures of the important documents and replaced everything. Moreover, the clue about her phone being destroyed meant she sent the pics to someone at her company and there is no way for the authorities to trace it. Cynthia committed the perfect crime. Rose had only one concern: who will be the lawyer to prosecute this case? She knew some lawyers in Nevada. Hopefully it will be one of our friends. Her goal was to settle out of court and that's why Cynthia told her to bring some money.

Chapter Nine
| The Last Night In Vegas |

Rose called Greg. It was Wednesday night around 1am. Greg rolled over and grabbed his cell phone. "Hello." Greg muttered groggy. Priscilla started to wake up. "Master Greg." Rose addressed, "It's Rose from Cynthia's place." "Hey Mrs. Rose," Greg was concerned, "you ok?" "Yes, I'm fine thank you," Rose answered, "but Cynthia and Tasha were arrested. They're in jail." "They're in jail!?" Greg blurted out surprised. Priscilla heard him and asked, "Who's in jail?" "Yes, I'm flying out tonight to bail them out." Rose stated, "It's a breaking and entering charge. It won't stick, but it could do some damage to Cynthia's reputation as the head of her company. Something tells me you and Priscilla should jump on a flight to Vegas as well to see about Tasha. I will bail both of them out. My flight leaves at 3am and I should arrive in Vegas between 7am - 7:30am. Call me when you get to Vegas." "Thank you Mrs. Rose," Greg said, "we will call you when we get there. Good bye." "Priscilla we are going to Vegas." Greg announced, "Cynthia and Tasha have been arrested and put in jail on charges of breaking and entering." Priscilla booked a flight for two to Vegas immediately. They were to leave at 10:38am. The couple started packing in preparation to leave Atlanta.

"There goes a good night sleep." Priscilla remarked. "Babydoll, we can sleep on the plane." Greg shared, "how long is the flight?" Priscilla checked, "It's about 4 hours and 17 mins." "You know

Greg, this smells like one of Cynthia's scams to me." Priscilla speculated, "I bet you I'm right. It has something to do with her corporation. I pray Tasha doesn't get hurt behind this." "This is my fault." Greg replied, "I never made the call to Tasha when you warned me about Cynthia, I forgot." "No. Everyone is responsible for their own actions." Priscilla clarified, "Let's just get there and see what we can do to help." Greg and Cynthia made it to the airport and boarded their flight. They slept like babies on the airplane. They arrived in Vegas at around 11:55am Vegas time. Greg called Rose. "Hey Mrs. Rose we just landed," Greg informed her, "we are here in Vegas now. What is going on with the girls?" "I got the girls out of jail." Rose explained, "They are at their hotel now. I will text you the information. You and Priscilla should come and visit them now." "Ok," Greg responded, "we will get a cab. Be there shortly." They grabbed a cab and made their way to The Venetian Hotel. They went to the front desk and contacted the room. They were allowed to go up. Priscilla was impressed with the hotel. "Oh my Greg," Priscilla commented, "this place is beautiful. I wish you had taken me here." "Me too, me too." Greg replied, "This is my favorite hotel on the strip." They arrived at the floor and went to the door of the girl's room. Greg knocked and the door swung open. "Hey, you girls ok?" Greg asked. "Yeah, we are fine." Cynthia responded. Greg walked over to hug Tasha. It was a bit awkward with Greg traveling with Priscilla and Tasha being with Tony last night; well, the last two nights. "Hey baby." Tasha asked. "You good?" "Yes, I'm good. Just concerned about you. Rose added, "I have to meet with the other lawyers at 3pm today Master Greg." Rose detailed. "The other lawyers?" Greg asked feeling confused, "I don't understand what you mean, other lawyers?" "Ummm, Master Greg," Rose confessed, "I am a lawyer too. I am Cynthia's lawyer. I used to be a lawyer back in the military." "Sorry ma'am, I meant no disrespect," Greg apologized, "I didn't know. So how is the case looking so far?" "Greg, don't you worry your little head about this." Rose told him, "I'll have these fancy lawyers eating out of the palm of my hand before this is over. I'm trying to make it so we don't have to go to court. We will settle out of court if everything goes our way. Priscilla, I need you to come with me." "Ok," Priscilla responded humbly. They left to meet the other lawyers.

"Can you girls tell me what happened from the very beginning?" Greg asked. "It's nothing," Cynthia assured him, "we were in this guy's room and I opened his safe while he was uhhh pre-occupied. I took some pictures of some documents and we left. I sent the pictures to my company, and I destroyed the phone. We were arrested for opening the safe." "What were you doing in this guy's room?" Greg asked getting more and more upset at Cynthia, "And who was this dude anyway? Did you know him Tasha?" Tasha was feeling so guilty now that Greg was here. "No.., no.., no..," Tasha was stuttering. "No, she doesn't know him Greg." Cynthia explained, "I know him. He's a business associate of mine. And he invited us up." "Up where?" Greg continued asking questions. He didn't feel like he had the whole story. "He was staying at the Bellagio in a penthouse suite." Cynthia replied. "A penthouse suite.

Do you know how much that costs?" Greg noted being surprised. "I know," Cynthia said, "but it's over now Greg. There is no problem. My mom will take care of the lawyers and we will be back in Hotlanta tomorrow." "Your mom!!??" Greg asked. "Rose is my mom." Cynthia told him. "Are you kidding me?!" Greg exclaimed, "I didn't know I was speaking to your mom all those conversations that she and I shared." "Shared about what?" Cynthia questioned genuinely interested. "About nothing and different things." Greg dodged the question. "We don't have secrets here Greg," Cynthia advised, "I just told you the whole story. How a business acquaintance of mine invited us up to his penthouse suite at the Bellagio for a meal, and I took pictures of some documents that my company needed. I destroyed the evidence and got out of there. No problem. Tasha was never in any danger. She didn't even know what I was doing or why I was doing it. So everything is fine here. You didn't need to come." "Hmmm," Greg murmured partially satisfied. "Why did you bring Priscilla with you?" Tasha asked feeling a little jealous. "Ahhhum.., well..," Greg started out slowly, but Cynthia interrupted him. "...No, that was me. I hired her to watch over Greg while we were gone." Cynthia confessed. Greg kept his mouth closed. Maybe Cynthia could talk him out of this mess. "That is crazy." Tasha indicated, "Greg is a big boy. He doesn't need anyone to hold his hand." "Oh come on Tash." Cynthia pleaded, "Let Greg have his fun while we are off having our fun in Vegas. Right? Live and let live. So he had a couple of strippers dance for him when we were out of town. What's the big deal? An eye for an eye, right? You have your fun and he has his fun. Everyone is happy in our threesome. Right Tash?" Tasha could read between the lines quite well; especially with her guilty conscience. She clearly understood what Cynthia was saying. Namely that you have been cheating on him so let him have his fun with the stripper girls; live and let live. She didn't want to push it any further, and acquiesced giving in peacefully. "Right, right." Tasha consented. Now that Greg was there, Cynthia wanted Greg to do it to her bad. She felt like he wasn't mad at her anymore and Tasha had been having all the fun sexually on this Vegas trip. She started making plans to have him in her bed tonight.

Rose and Priscilla headed to the meeting with the lawyers. Rose explained to Priscilla that she knew the prosecutor personally, and she might be able to settle out of court. "His name is Craig Newton." Rose explained, "We served together in the military. He is the lead lawyer on this case. He is working his way up the ladder to be the D.A. Therefore, it is very important to him to win every case." "When we get there in the room, I want you to pose as my assistant. These guys need to be distracted by your beauty so I can work my magic. All you got to do is smile and agree with me. Oh, and be distractingly beautiful which you do in your sleep. We will have them eating out of the palms of our hand's young lady." Rose smiled at Priscilla.

The meeting room was set up in a simple manner. There was a rectangular table in the center of the room. One side of the table had three chairs, and on the other side of the table had two chairs.

Rose sat in one of the two chairs and Priscilla sat in the other. On the other side of the table sat Craig Newton, there was Jerry Toliver a young whipper snapper of a lawyer who's eager and aggressive, and finally there was Mr. Andrews. Mr. Andrews was the client and represents Tru-Max. Rose started the conversation, "Gentlemen, thank you for granting us this meeting. We think there can be a quick and fair resolution of this case. First of all, my clients did not steal anything or even damage anything. They are just two girls out to have a little fun in Vegas. No harm, no foul." "No harm, no foul!?" Jerry Toliver exclaimed disgusted, "are you kidding me? We are talking about top secret information has been stolen. This will lead to billions of dollars in loss for our client Tru-Max." "I'm sorry," Rose said politely, "what proof do you have that information was stolen?" "Well, why do you think the safe was opened?" Mr. Toliver asked. "As a lawyer, you should know you don't answer a question with a question Mr. Toliver." Rose corrected him, "Again, I will pose the question: what proof do you have that information was stolen?" "I have none." Mr. Toliver responded. "There is no real crime committed here." Rose explained, "We are willing to settle this out of court which will be better for both parties." "Rose..., Rose..., Rose...," Craig Newton uttered slowly, "our client is not interested in settling out of court. You know as well as I do Cynthia Heart has cost our client millions of dollars; no billions of dollars. Off the record, they want her head on a platter, and there is nothing on this planet you can do to change it." "Ok, off the record," Rose continued, "so this is about revenge clear and simple. Well Craig you got nothin.' Cynthia didn't break any laws. You will never get a conviction. There is no evidence." "She didn't break any laws?" Craig asked, "What do you think opening a safe that doesn't belong to you is? It is a crime in the state of Nevada Rose, a crime." "A misdemeanor?" Rose detailed, "Really Craig? These guys hired you, a top lawyer in this town, to prosecute my daughter for a misdemeanor. How much are they paying you for prosecuting Cynthia Heart for a misdemeanor? Tru-Max is a trillion-dollar business that's paying you insane amounts of money to prosecute Cynthia for a misdemeanor. Mr. Andrews tell me it isn't so. Craig you might as well get her for jaywalking. That is going to look really good on your record, prosecuting people for misdemeanors, woooo hoooo. Craig is a crack pot lawyer. Look at all those misdemeanors. You are pathetic." "I forgot how good you are Rose," Craig commented, "but it doesn't matter we are not budging. We are going to prosecute your daughter, whether it's for a felony or a misdemeanor." "Ok, I can see this is getting us nowhere." Rose replied disappointed, "Craig, can I have a word with you in private?" "If you think it will help." Craig responded. "I do." Rose replied.

The two of them stepped out of the room into the hallway. Priscilla couldn't help herself. She was completely at home with these types of powerful men. They didn't intimidate her at all. "Do you mind if I get some coffee?" Priscilla said innocently. "Help yourself." Mr. Toliver said. He had been eyeing her the whole time. She knew he was attracted to her. She decided to give those guys a show just for the hell of it. The coffee station was directly behind her chair. She stood up, turned around, took a step or two towards the coffee table, and dropped her pen. Priscilla was wearing a tight-fitting skirt and a white shirt. It was very professional attire, but she made it look good. She slowly bent over bending her knees slightly to grab her pen very slowly. She slowly stood back up. Priscilla paused momentarily, and turned her head towards the two men. They were staring. She asked naively, "What? Why are you looking at me?" Priscilla thought to herself, 'Men are so easy to control.'

Meanwhile, out in the hallway, things were not going so good for Rose. "Look Rose," Craig explained, "this thing is going down. My client has it out for Cynthia." "Ok," Rose replied, "stand back a little. I want to show you something." "What?" Craig asked not understanding what it could be. "Step back," Rose repeated, "I want to show you a video I have on my phone." Craig stepped back with a smirk. Rose held her phone up sideways, pressed a button on the screen, and a video started playing. Craig watched intently for a moment. She took the phone back and put it in her purse. "Blackmail, really?" Craig asked thoughtfully, "Ya know, I never seen you lose a case Rose. No one is that good." "It's not blackmail," Rose detailed, "I'm willing to pay so we can settle out of court. It's not blackmail Craig. I just want you to know I will visit your wife immediately after this meeting and I will tell her about our little rendezvous. How you stuck it in me so hard and deep that I screamed. Remember? Of course, you have to understand the context of that scream. It was a scream of delight, but I will probably leave that detail out when I tell the story to your wife in a few minutes. She is meeting me for a bite to eat not far from here. Let's just settle this out of court and call it a day. Subsequently, I will have pleasant things to say to your wife Craig. I really like her." "You would ruin my marriage over this?" Craig asked. "No, I wouldn't," Rose told him, "but evidently you would. Your secret is safe with me. I don't kiss and tell Craig. However, you are not taking my daughter down. Go in there and convince your client it would be more beneficial to settle out of court than drag Cynthia Heart through the mud. I'm willing to pay one and a half. What's your commission on this Craig? Pretty good for not prosecuting a case don't you think. This can be over in a few minutes and we can all go home. In addition, you can go home to a loving wife with a lot more cheddar in your pocket. Don't be a fool Craig." "Ok, let me see what I can do." Craig says as they both re-entered the room. Craig pulled his client and fellow lawyer into the corner of the room and begin explaining why it's better to settle than to drag this case through court. It took some convincing, but his marriage was on the line. After about 10 minutes the three men returned to the table. Craig didn't say a word. He took a sheet of paper, folded it in half, and wrote a number on it. He slid it over to Rose. She peaked at it and looked at Craig. She didn't say a word. Rose grabbed her laptop and opened it. She slid the paper back to Craig which read, "Account number?" He wrote down the account number and slid the paperback to Rose. After a bunch of clicking and tapping it was done. "Check the account right now." Rose suggested. Mr. Andrews looked on his phone and nodded to Rose. "I take it you will file this settlement with the court system? Gentlemen, it was a pleasure." Rose responded as she gathered her things and left with Priscilla. "Priscilla," Rose informed her, "Sometimes it's good to be bad." "Mrs. Rose, you got to tell me what you did to change Craig's mind." Priscilla asked smiling, "You are truly badass. Pardon my French."

Cynthia entered the hotel room explaining the activities for the girls' last night in Vegas. She told Tasha she called the party girls Tammy and Lynn. They agreed to come to their room so everyone would go together to this club where they would dance, drink, and party down. "They will be here in an hour or so," Cynthia shared, "do you know what you are going to wear?" "Ummm, I'll wear my blue party dress," Tasha said, "but what about Greg? What will he do?" "Well, I had Rose get him a room for the night here at The Venetian." Cynthia explained, "He can hang with Rose and Priscilla, or maybe grab some dinner and a show possibly." "Cynthia, you think of everything girl." Tasha identified, "Greg, it's our last night in Vegas. We are going to have some fun. Tomorrow we return to Atlanta and I will be yours again. Ok? Babe don't be mad." "I'm totally fine with it." Greg confessed, "You girls have a blast and I will get some dinner, or maybe catch a show."

Greg was still hanging around the room when the party girls arrived. "This is Greg." Tasha introduced him to her new friends. "Greg this is Tammy and Lynn." "Pleased to meet you ladies." Greg replied. "Mmmm," Tammy whispered to Tasha, "I want some of that." "This is my boyfriend girl," Tasha told her, "he is letting me go out one last time for "Girls Night" with you all." "Girl, you got good taste." Tammy indicated. "Everyone ready?" Lynn asked. "Yeah, I'm ready," Tasha replied. "Girls, I'm not feeling so well," Cynthia informed, "you all go without me this time. If I feel better later, I will call you and catch up with you." "Ok, no problem. We will take real good care of your partner in crime." Tammy added, "We will escort her back here when we are finished partying." "Thanks girls," Cynthia said, "have a blast!!" The party crew left and headed to the club. "Wow, I'm feeling better already Greg," Cynthia uttered with a wicked smile, "let's order something to eat." Greg and Cynthia hung out in the room while the girls were out partying.

After eating a meal, Cynthia made a phone call away from Greg. She came back in the room with Greg and asked, "Did I show you the hot tub they have here in this room?" She walked him to the bathroom with the hot tub and directed him, "Get in it with me babe." She undressed Greg and he entered the hot tub. She took off her clothes and joined him. Cynthia smiled and told Greg she really missed him. She moved to him and sat in his lap. The hot water was beading down her breasts as Greg gazed. The water was very soothing with the massaging jets relaxing their muscles. Cynthia had her arms around Greg and started kissing him. Greg knew where this was going. He wasn't mad at her. He just stopped trusting her. He became accustomed to making out with her and even making love to her. She was now like an old girlfriend to him. There was a knock at the door. "Someone's at the door," Cynthia said, "Stay put I'll get it." She jumps out of the hot tub, put on a robe, and ran to the door. "Mmmm, Greg look what I found at the door?" Cynthia expressed as she led Priscilla into the bathroom, "I found a little treat for you." Greg swung his head around only to see Priscilla dressed in a sexy school girl outfit. She had a very short sexy plaid skirt on with a white button-down shirt that was tied at the bottom to reveal her flat midsection. "She's hot." Cynthia narrated, "With her smooth brown skin, her dark brown eyes, her big shapely behind, and those fat juicy titties. Greg, we have a toy we can play with. I've never seen you screw a call girl before. There is a rumor going around that you make them orgasm. Is this true?" "Cynthia," Greg said in a serious tone, "let this girl go back to her room." "No." She replied. "I'm paying her good money Greg to service your needs. That's her job. Now it's time for her to perform her end of the contract." "I want you to make her orgasm in front of me." Cynthia lustfully stated, "Hell, why would anyone make a call girl orgasm? Shouldn't they be getting you off? Not vice versa." This situation had become a power struggle in front of Priscilla. Greg decided to end it. He got out of the hot tub naked and grabbed Cynthia's hand. As he left the bathroom, he grabbed a towel. "Cynthia," Greg conversed, "this is crazy. Don't drag this innocent girl into our relationship. I know you are powerful. I know you control these call girls which work for you. However, you are playing a game with other people's lives and it's just not right." "Oh, you know your falling for her." Cynthia fired back, "I see the way you look at her, and don't think I didn't notice that little necklace Priscilla is wearing everywhere she goes now. I know my girls

Greg. Priscilla does not wear jewelry unless the job calls for it. She doesn't have tattoos. She doesn't even smoke. Now after a week with you she has this gorgeous heart necklace. You can read me? I can read you and her. Fuck her in front of me to humiliate her and I will send her back to her room." "Oh wow," Greg couldn't believe it, "again you can't make this stuff up. Is this you being jealous? You are jealous of a low-level call girl at the club. You are a millionaire, the most powerful woman I have ever seen in my life, and you are jealous of a hooker? This girl is nothing to you. How can she be so important to you?" "Come here," Greg pulled her close to him, "you know how I feel about you, don't you? I know how you feel about me. We don't need any other people in our relationship. I promise to give you love tonight like you have never received before, if you will do me a simple favor. Let Priscilla go back to her room right now. Do we have a deal?" "Ok," Cynthia said, "we have deal. Priscilla! Come here dear." "Yes," Priscilla replied. "We are going to let you go back to your room now." Cynthia told her. "Yes ma'am." Priscilla answered heading to the door rather quickly. "Wait a moment," Cynthia called out, "I need you to leave my property here with me before you go." "What?" Greg couldn't believe what he was hearing. "They're my clothes," Cynthia indicated, "I paid for them. She needs to take them off and leave them with me. Then she can leave. I'm still honoring our deal Greg." "No problem." Priscilla affirmed. She took off the top and she removed the skirt. She placed them on the couch. Priscilla was topless with a tiny pair of white panties on. She opened the door and left. "Wow," Greg uttered in disbelief, "you got to be kidding me." "Ahhh, its ok." Cynthia responded, "She's a big girl and I'm paying her very well. She'll be fine. Just her pride is bruised…"

In the hallway Priscilla was covering her breasts and looking for someone to help her. She saw a couple get off the elevator. She asked them to help her contact Rose. The young couple gave her a towel from their room and let her use their phone to call Rose. Rose came quickly and brought the girl some clothes. Priscilla thanked the couple.

"…Now you have to keep your end of the deal mister." Cynthia told him smiling. "Where were we…?"

Meanwhile, Tammy, Lynn, and Tasha finally arrived to the club. The music was blasting and they were trying to find a table to sit down to order some drinks to get started. Tammy led the girls to a table where there was a guy already sitting. His back was to them. Tasha declared, "We can't sit here girl. This guy was here first." "No," Tammy explained, "he's holding the table for us." "Really? Who is this guy?" Tasha asked. Right then the gentleman turned around and looked Tasha in the face. "Tangela," Tony called, "how are you?" She was stunned. She didn't know how to play this. Surely he knew her real name. He was the reason they were thrown in jail. How does he know these girls? Tasha didn't have a game plan she was frozen. She didn't speak. "Come on Tasha." Tony named her playfully, "You remember me? It's only been one day." Now Tasha was angry. She knew he knew everything, yet he was trying to act like nothing happened. "YOU PRICK!!!!!" Tasha exclaimed, "You are the reason we were thrown in jail! Nothing was taken from the safe! We settled for 1.5 million! And you think you can just show up out of the blue and everything is going to be fine between us? Anyway, who told you we were going to be here? What is going on Tony?" "1.5 million," Tammy asked surprised, "WTF! Nobody said anything about that kind of money." "Tasha…," Tony spoke slowly, "…let's sit down… and I will… explain everything." "No," Tasha replied, "you will explain everything right here right now." "Ok," Tony started off, "I didn't call the police. I had to report the safe was opened. That's company policy. Corporate security called the hotel security, and had the police arrest you guys. But you weren't honest with me either. You were working with Cynthia Heart our biggest competitor. She wants our secrets. She needs our secrets. And I am surprised they settled for 1.5 million. That is very, very, cheap for the kind of money Cynthia deals in. There has to be something more to the story. Tasha, I missed you. I need you and I will do whatever it takes to make it up to you. Just tell me what I need to do to make this right. My company's issues with Cynthia have nothing to do with you and I. In fact, believe it or not, it was Cynthia who let me know where you would be this evening. There…, I have told you everything." "Oh my, my, my," Tammy said, "he's fine and rich and that was a pretty good apology Tasha. Believe me I'm an expert on apologies. I think we should sit with him and hear some more. Besides, he said he would do anything you want him to do." She looked directly at Tasha and winked. She was indicating they could use him to party. The guy is filthy rich after all. Tasha couldn't transition from angry to happy fast, but maybe she could get a few drinks in her and she would feel differently. So they all sat down and ordered drinks. Tasha was pretty quiet trying to digest all of this. What was Cynthia thinking in setting Tony up with us girls? Is that why she didn't come?

Tammy and Lynn were having the time of their lives. They were dancing, drinking, and laughing. They even got Tony up to dance a couple of times. Tasha just sat there nursing her drink thinking. "Tasha," Tony said, "talk to me. What is going through your head right now? You are so quiet just sitting there. Tonight you should have some fun." "Hmmm…, …really?" Tasha questioned, "Then tell me something Tony. Why are you here?" "I'm here to see you." Tony explained, "Cynthia told me you are leaving tomorrow, and maybe I will never see you again." "Ok, if you never see me again," Tasha asked, "would that be a problem?" "Absolutely," Tony responded, "I don't want to live without you. I know we got off on the wrong foot. I know you can't decide if I'm the enemy or your friend right now. But last night was magic. It was special for me. I know you felt the same way too. I felt it in the last couple of kisses we shared." "You kissed this guy?" Tammy asked a little drunk, "A couple of times even?" "Tony, you can have any girl you want." Tasha pointed out, "Why are you interested in me? It was a one night stand. A chance encounter. We are like two ships passing in the night. Two people who will never see each other again." "That's ridiculous Tasha." Tony stated, "There is an invention that you must not have heard of. It's called a cell phone. You punch in numbers to talk to anyone anywhere. Listen, there is no such thing as two people who will never see each other again." "Now you are a comedian." Tasha replied. "Who among you have seen the Vegas strip at night from a limousine?" Tony asked. "Does the limousine have a liquor bar in it?" Lynn asked. "Not only does it have a liquor bar, it also has several handsome eligible bachelors from my company who have nothing to do tonight." Tony baited the girls. "We are there Tony," Tammy replied, "you don't have to ask twice."

Tony had his limo go up and down the strip so the girls could see Vegas and have a blast. The gentlemen from his company were quite handsome and a lot of fun. After touring the strip for about an hour, the limo pulled up to the Bellagio. Everyone got out and Tony announced, "I have a surprise for Tammy and Lynn." "Do tell, do tell." Lynn said excited. "I have a luxury penthouse suite here at the Bellagio," Tony explained, "and I found out the penthouse suite across the hall from mine is vacant for the night. So I rented it for you two to enjoy. We will party here at the Bellagio. Then you can go up to your room and enjoy it. Let's all go up so I can show you your room." "Girl I died and went to heaven." Tammy proclaimed, "Pinch me. I must be dreaming!" They all went up to see the penthouse suite for the girls. The girls were completely spellbound. "Shoot! We could have the party right here." Lynn suggested, "We don't have to go back down stairs." "Sure," Tony replied, "you can have the wait staff supply you with alcohol and food or whatever you need. Just tell them to put it on Tony's tab. My name carries a little weight around here." "Tony you are too kind," Tammy gratefully expressed, "I'm leaving you my number just in case you ever come to Cincinnati, Ohio. Just call us we got you."

Tony took Tasha's hand and led her out of the room. They walked down the hall to Tony's penthouse suite and entered. Tony reminded Tasha, "There is something we started that we have to finish tonight." The girls had to cover for Tasha. They were supposed to bring her back to her hotel after partying. However, it looks like she will be spending the night at the Bellagio with Tony who they know for sure is not her boyfriend. "What do we do?" Lynn asked Tammy. "Uhhhh, I got it." Tammy responded, "We will call Cynthia now. We tell her we are going to crash at our hotel and we will bring Tasha back in the morning." And that's what they did.

Cynthia told Greg Tasha was staying with the party girls until morning. "Good," Cynthia said, "I got you all to myself. I don't have to share you." They were in the hot tub again. This time there was no distraction. Cynthia was straddling Greg. She was splashing water as she went up and down on his sturdy penis, while steadying herself by holding on to the edge of the hot tub. They were having fun while trying to keep the water in the tub...

...Things started to heat up back at the Bellagio. Tasha and Tony were hugging and kissing in the living room. Tasha wasn't quite sure what her game plan was this time. She was alone. There was no Cynthia to influence her behavior. For the first time in a long time, Tasha had to make a decision on her own. She knew tonight was the last night in Vegas. She was going to do what she wanted to do. Right now, on this last night in Vegas, she wanted to make love to Tony. "Tony, this is just for tonight." Tasha whispered, "Don't get any permanent ideas." "If this is just for tonight," Tony said, "you have to give me your all. Agreed?" "Agreed," Tasha whispered. He led her to the bed. He sat down on the bed and Tasha started to undo her dress so that it fell to the floor. "My, my, my, Tasha," Tony admitted, "you have never looked so good to a man." "Could you help me with my panties?" Tasha asked teasing him. He pulled them to the floor and she gingerly stepped out of them. Tasha felt like a precious angel around Tony. She helped him get undressed. He was already fully erect. She pushed him back onto the bed and did something a little different for her. She remembered what Cynthia told her. There has to be a give and take in a sexual relationship. Tasha took Tony's dick into her mouth and stimulated the hell out of it. She started slowly. She increased in speed and intensity little by little. Tony was loving it. He leaned back with his hands under is head and tried to absorb all of the pleasure without orgasming in her mouth. Right before he climaxed, Tony grabbed Tasha and pulled her toward him. She was trying to sit on him, but Tony turned and rolled her on her back. He hovered over her breathing deeply. He passionately kissed her for a very long time, and finally slid himself inside her. She moaned a little as entered her. He started slow while looking deep into her light brown eyes. Tony was actually making love to Tasha and Tasha could feel it. He measured his every move. Tony wanted to impress her and make her never forget this moment. His pace quickened slightly.

His thrusts became more deliberate and more pronounced. Tasha was falling for him. She did the unthinkable. Tasha crossed a line. A line that should never be crossed unless you are going to stay with the person. She told him she would give him her all tonight. Tony stopped to reposition Tasha's sexy body. He pulled her to the edge of the bed by sliding her across those silk sheets. It felt so good to Tasha. It was like she was in a dreamworld with Tony. Tony spread her legs and stood over her like he was her king. Then the penetration began slow at first. Tasha loved it. Until this point, neither of them talked much during their sexual connection. Tony was inspired to tell Tasha what was on his heart. "Baby," Tony said, "I don't want to live without you. I need you to know this." "I understand," Tasha replied sweetly. "You tell me what to do and I will do it." Tony continued, "I'm convinced you are perfect for me and I am perfect for you. Anything you want . . ." He tapered off as he was putting in some hard work on Tasha. "Come here." Tasha told Tony as she moved to the center of the bed, "Lie on your back. It's my turn now." She mounted him, grabbed his erection, and slid down slowly. She started working her hips. Tasha loved being on top. She could direct and control things. She could bounce up and down. She could go back and forth or she could go round and round. She could do whatever she wanted on top, and the bonus was Tony loved Tasha's breasts. Or should we say Kassandra and Tangela's titties? Tony already had both of them sexually in his penthouse suite, but now he has the real woman. No false names, no one coaching, and no secret drugs involved. Tony was in ecstasy. Tasha's full breasts were in clear view of Tony now. They were dancing and jiggling right before his eyes. He was hypnotized. The man was being satisfied on several different levels at the same time. He was in 7th heaven….

…Greg had Cynthia bent over the hot tub. He held her by the elbows doggystyle. Cynthia had no control. Greg was in complete control penetrating her deeper as he pulled her towards him with his arms. Subconsciously, Greg was punishing her for the mistreatment of his little flower Priscilla. He was not overtly mad at Cynthia, but inside he was righting a wrong by the way he was having sex with her. Next position was similar, he took one of her legs and put it over his shoulder. Cynthia was bent over and her weight was resting on one leg and her hand was on the wall of the hot tub. He was in total control and she held on for dear life. From Cynthia's point of view the sex was great. She just wanted his attention. She was tired of being in the dog house. She just wanted Tasha out of the way, and on this night in Vegas, she was happy as she could be having Greg alone with her. She was living Greg's promised gift to Tasha. A romantic encounter at The Venetian in Vegas.

Cynthia loved Greg's attention. She loved anything Greg wanted to do to her. Cynthia was silly in love with Greg like a little girl. She was his willing play toy. She would do whatever he said. Greg was the only person who could control Cynthia. His problem was that he always underestimated her. She was always crazier than he could even imagine. Cynthia was always a step ahead of him; always.

The party girls, Tammy and Lynn, had a blast in their penthouse suite. They stayed up all night partying, drinking, and laughing, but they had a mission. They still had to return Tasha to her hotel room. Around 8:30am they dragged themselves out of bed and knocked on Tony's door. "Yeah, good morning." Tammy said, "Hate to wake you, but we got to take Tasha back to her hotel. Is she decent?" "Oh yeah, good morning. Come on in." Tony told them. He was in his robe, "Tasha is in the shower. She will be out in a minute. So how was your night?" "Simply the best night ever," Lynn declared, "thank you Tony. You are the best." "We ate, we drank, we sang, we danced, and we had a blast." Tammy described, "I tell you, we will never forget the generosity and kindness you showed us Tony. Please call us if you are ever in Ohio. You are family now." Tasha came in the living room wearing a white robe. "Good morning party girls!!" Tasha greeted, "How was the penthouse suite?" "Are you kidding? You have to ask?" Lynn asked, "We had a blast!" "I'm glad." Tasha expressed, "Give me a second to put on some clothes and I will be ready to go." Tasha gathered her things together and she kissed Tony goodbye. As she walked away, he grabbed her and pulled her into his personal space. He whispered something in her ear and kissed her again. The party girls were impressed by the intense display of affection from Tony. They started talking about it as they were leaving the Bellagio.

"Somebody going to miss you a lot." Tammy commented smiling, "How is it you have two boyfriends and I can't even get one?" "Don't remind me, please? I don't want to think about it right now." Tasha answered. "Greg is a nice choice, and Tony is even a nicer choice." Lynn conveyed, "I don't think you can choose wrong either way you go. I'm just saying." They took Tasha back to her room at The Venetian. They kissed and hugged, said their goodbyes, and the girls left Tasha there with Cynthia and Greg.

"You good?" Cynthia asked looking intently into the eyes of Tasha for a sign. "I'm good." Tasha responded like a robot, "The girls and I had a great time last night." "What did y'all do?" Greg asked. "We went to the club and partied there for a while," Tasha recounted, "then we got a limo and went up and down the Vegas strip. After that they, we, just partied some more and we were bushed so we went to bed." "That was wild," Greg replied, "those girls can really party huh?" "You can say that again." Tasha admitted. Cynthia was not convinced. She knew she set Tasha up with Tony. She wanted to know what really happened. Greg invited the two girls down to grab some breakfast. They told him to go down first, get a table, and they would join him later.

"You can start eating Greg," Cynthia told him, "I know you are hungry. We will be down in a little bit." Greg hung up. "Tasha, do tell." Cynthia stated with excitement in her voice, "What happened with Tony?" "So you told him we were coming to that club?" Tasha asked, "Why? What were you trying to do?" "Listen Tasha," Cynthia explained, "I got you in to this whole mess in the first place. I didn't know you and Tony would hit it off. But I saw you kiss him when we were leaving. There was definitely something there. He likes you and you like him. So for your last night in Vegas, I thought I would put you two together. Tell me what happened." "Ok, Tony got us a limo so we could see the strip." Tasha shared, "He had some guys from his office there to entertain Tammy and Lynn, and they were having a great time with those guys. We then went to the Bellagio. Tony paid for a penthouse suite for Tammy and Lynn to stay the night. They partied, ate, and drank and everything else. Tony and I went to his penthouse suite to be alone together." "And!!!?" Cynthia asked with anticipation, "What happened?" "Uhhhh," Tasha sighed, "we made love all night. I forgot about Greg temporarily and we connected on a level. I crossed a line. I'm afraid I lost myself. I was loving this guy with all my might. I gave myself to him completely; not just my naked body. I gave this man my soul. I can't stop thinking about him." "What about him?" Cynthia solicited, "Was he playing you girl? Was he fucking you? I know for a fact he loves your tits. Was he making love to you Tash? You were paying attention, right?" "I know for a fact he was making love to me." Tasha asserted, "We were both gone. It was special... It was magic... It was super powerful. It was a fairy tale love affair." "Ok..., there is just one question left girl...," Cynthia requested, "do you trust me?" "Of course." "Then I put you under oath." Cynthia probed, "You must tell me the absolute and total truth." "Ok." Tasha answered. "Which one do you love the most?" Cynthia asked as she stared deep into Tasha's eyes. There was an uncomfortable silence which filled the room. A pause you could feel deep down in your bones. Cynthia yells, "Tony! Oh my God girl it's Tony!" "I didn't say that." Tasha replied. "Your silence said it. I heard it in the silence crystal clear." Cynthia emphasized, "Home girl you are in trouble. You are committed to one man, but currently in love with another." "I will never see him again." Tasha retorted confidently. "I told him it was our last night together." "And what did he say?" Cynthia asked quickly. "Uhhhh, if it is our last night, you have to give me your all tonight." Tasha replied with a little embarrassment. Cynthia burst out laughing. "And that is exactly what you did, isn't it? You gave Tony your all. Didn't you?" "Yeah, but it was our last time." Tasha tried to sound reasonable. "I won't see him ever again thankfully." "When you love with all of your heart, it is never the last time." Cynthia detailed. "Love can only grow when you express it. If it is true love. Ok? You don't know Tony." "That's right," Tasha replied, "I don't know Tony. Therefore how can I love someone I don't know? I don't love Tony." "Tasha, you can love someone you don't know." Cynthia assured her, "It happens every day. I said you don't know him to make the point that this guy is not going away. I know Tony. I've known him for 10 years. He doesn't go away. He doesn't quit. If this man is hunting you - if this man decides he wants you - you are as good as his." "Don't say that," Tasha begged, "I'm Greg's. I belong to Greg. It doesn't matter how I feel about Tony." Silence once again surrounded the ladies ending their conversation. The girls went down stairs to join Greg for breakfast. Tasha was noticeably quiet and preoccupied. Greg picked up on it, but didn't say anything. He figured they would talk about it later. After they finished eating, they returned to pack their things and went to the airport. Everyone caught their flights and went back to Atlanta on Thursday.

Greg knew he wouldn't see Priscilla again. It was like ripping off a band-aid. The faster the better so they could both get over each other and move on. However, Greg was still determined to help Priscilla. He was keeping his eye out for a young gentleman that was worthy of her love. Greg wanted to see her loved and adored.

Tasha called Cynthia when she got home Thursday night. "Don't forget your promise," Tasha reminded her, "you got to give the money back to Jessica." "Don't worry. I will do it tomorrow." Cynthia responded, "I will go to the bank and get it out. Then I will swing by the job and give it to her." "What are you going to tell her?" Tasha asked. "I'll tell her I had a private detective watching the bench that I left the money at," Cynthia explained, "and he followed the guy that retrieved the money. He followed him back to his place. When the guy who retrieved the money left his house, the private detective went in the house, grabbed the money, the video recording. and left. I will give her the money and the video recording, and all is well." "Ok," Tasha smiled, "that works."

Tasha, Cynthia, and Greg took Friday off from work. It was the day for them to enjoy their threesome. Tasha was afraid Greg would be able to see she wasn't making love to him with all of her heart. She was guilty; or at least she had a guilty conscience. As for Cynthia, for the first time she was not planning ahead. She was just watching and waiting. Cynthia knew the relationship between Tasha and Greg was in jeopardy. She knew Tony was coming and either Greg would find out Tasha slept with Tony, or Tasha would find out Greg slept with the stripper girls; most notably, Priscilla. Cynthia was in the wait and see mode. She figured within one week all hell would break loose. Tasha and Greg came to Paradise in the afternoon around 4pm. Cynthia suggested they stretch out on the couch and watch some movies. She thought Greg would take one of them upstairs and the other would continue watching movies. When he was done, he would take the other girl upstairs. It really didn't matter to her at this point. By the way, that is exactly what happened, Greg tapped Tasha on the shoulder and indicated to her he wanted to take her upstairs. An electric shock of fear ran through her body. She was trying to be cool. Cynthia was looking her dead in the face to see her reaction. Cynthia knew there was trouble in Paradise. She smiled to herself.

Greg brought her into the room and he began to undress her. She was shivering from his touch. "Baby, you are cold." He said, "Do you want to keep some clothes on?" "No," Tasha replied, "I'm good." The love making started. Greg was methodical. He knew what she liked. Tasha preferred it slow so he gave it to her slow. He noticed her reaction was slightly different. So he thought, 'Maybe she wants me to speed it up a little.' He began to penetrate her faster. Not too fast, but noticeably faster. Her breathing increased, but she didn't say anything. Greg tried something else. He rolled her on her stomach and laid on her. He drove it up inside of her from the back. He got a little rise out of her so he continued. Next, he turned her over. Now she was facing him. He took her ankles and put them on his shoulder. He was going to make her climax. Tasha was unaware of what he was about to do. She had no warning. Greg pushed and thrusted trying to find the correct angle to enter her where he could stimulate the inside and the outside of the pussy at the same time. Finally, she started moaning in pleasure. This is always a good sign. Greg continued and he penetrated more diligently. The moans became louder and finally she had an orgasm. It felt so good to her that she couldn't help but say, "Oh Tony!" "What the . . . !!!" Greg was furious. He rolled over and jumped out of the bed. He turned on the lights and looked at Tasha, "Who's Tony?" "Nobody," Tasha said petrified, "nobody." "Nobody? Why did you just say his name if he's a nobody?" Greg demanded. "Baby get back in the bed." Tasha pleaded, "I'm sorry. It was just a slip of the lip." "A slip of the lip," Greg replied as he got dressed, "yeah, a slip of the lip. You must think I'm a fool." He stormed out of the room and headed straight to Cynthia downstairs. "Be very careful how you answer the next question." Greg dictated to Cynthia. "Greg, I hate when you say that to me." Cynthia objected. "What happened? Why are you so mad?" "I need someone tell me who Tony is!" Greg strongly stated, "Baby I know that you know, and I know that Tasha knows. Now it's time for me to know. Who is Tony?" Tasha put a robe on and was coming down the stairs. She looked at Cynthia and mouthed the words very distinctly, 'Don't tell him.' Cynthia really wanted to tell Greg, but she knew if she did she would lose Tasha's favor forever. Cynthia got up and ran to Tasha on the stairs. She whispered to Tasha, "You have tell him. Tell him the truth." "No. I can't" Tasha responded. "Tell him the truth," Cynthia advised, "and then ask him if he had sex with the strippers. We have no secrets." Tasha was mad as hell at the thought Greg slept with those beautiful strippers behind her back. She gathered herself to confess her sin to Greg first. Then she would do exactly what Cynthia told her to do, ask about the strippers. "I cheated on you when I was in Vegas." Tasha confessed, "I slept with a man named Tony." Greg put his head in his hands and started rubbing his forehead like he had a really bad headache. He was so angry he couldn't think straight. He decided it was better to leave the premises before he did something rash. He turned and started walking to the door. "I told you the truth." Tasha declared, "Now it's your turn. Did you sleep with those strippers from the club?" He stopped in his path. He knew what was up. It was very clear this was Cynthia's doing. She encouraged him to sleep with the strippers, then turned around and told Tasha. Honestly, Greg couldn't be mad at Cynthia. He was too angry with Tasha. "I told you the truth." Tasha repeated, "Be a man and tell me the truth." "Yes! I slept with those hookers!" Greg admitted, "But it meant nothing, and you know that. You on the other hand are very much into Tony to yell out his name during sex." "Cheating is cheating." Tasha asserted, "There are no degrees of cheating." "Yes Tasha," Greg countered, "there are degrees of cheating." Greg walked out of the front door. Rose was standing around the corner. She heard the whole thing. Cynthia went chasing after Greg and Tasha simply sat down on the couch wondering if there were degrees of cheating or not. She still felt guilty.

"I don't care you fucked the call girls." Cynthia reasoned, "I'm not mad. It's no big deal to me. I don't care about that. Greg wait! Don't go hear me out!" Greg stopped for a minute to listen to Cynthia. "What just happened needed to happen. You guys have to get passed this. She cheated on you. You cheated on her. Let's just call it even. Greg, I know you love her. That doesn't change, and I know she loves you too." "Cynthia," Greg asked, "who is this guy?" "Don't you worry about that Greg," Cynthia told him, "Tony is a guy with a dick who fucked your girlfriend. Do you think he is someone special? Do you think he's superman? No! Greg he's a man who was there when Tasha was alone and vulnerable. That's all. That is over. It's in the past. Today is a new day. Let it go." "Do you know this dude?" Greg continued questioning, "Cynthia…, tell me how she met this guy." "You are asking questions you don't want to know the answers to Greg." Cynthia assured him. "Au Contraire," Greg replied, "I definitely want to know the answer to the question."

At that moment the door to the house opened…, and Tasha appeared. She walked to Greg's car. She stared at him with tears streaming down her face. "What do you want to do?" Tasha asked, "Are you just going to leave or are we going to fix this? Do you remember your promise to me that first night?" "Where did you meet this guy?" Greg requested. "I met him in Vegas. I already told you." Tasha muttered through her tears. "Who set you up with this guy?" Greg continued to drill down deeper; he had a hunch. "He is a friend of mine," Cynthia confessed, "I know him from doing business with his corporation. He is a competitor of mine. I needed some papers he had in his safe. I asked Tasha to distract him while I took pictures." "I know the rest of the story." Greg surmised. "I was just having sex with him to keep him busy while she broke into the safe." Tasha explained like it would make a difference to Greg. "Come back inside and let's have a drink." Cynthia proposed. They went back inside and had some drinks. Cynthia spiked Tasha's drink which quickly put her to sleep in the living room. Greg kept drinking until he was very drunk. Once again Cynthia wanted Greg to herself. She led Greg down the hall to her bedroom and they had sex.

Well, this is the beginning of the end if Cynthia couldn't do something to save this threesome. Things were starting to fall apart and everyone could see it. Even if Greg and Tasha worked together to save their relationship, Cynthia would have to go. And even if they didn't work to save their relationship, Greg is really not interested in Cynthia. The wheels are coming off this whole threesome thing. There is no reason for this thing to continue, or so it appears at this moment.

Chapter Ten
| The Seduction |

After Friday's events, both Tasha and Greg had some soul searching to do. They both needed to think about what just happened and why it happened. On Saturday and Sunday, they didn't get together or even call each other. They both went to work Monday and Greg decided to catch up with Tasha after work. He left his job early to get to her job around the time she normally left. However, what he found at her job shocked him. He waited in the lobby for her to come down from work. Tasha got off the elevator, but before she could walk to the lobby, she was stopped by a guy standing right outside the elevator. Greg had a front row seat. "Tony!" Tasha exclaimed, "What are you doing here? I told you this was over between us." "I can't live without you," Tony replied, "I want you to come and be with me." "Are you crazy?" Tasha asked, "Don't come to my job. I'm in a relationship." "You are all alone in a relationship," Tony stated, "that's why you came into my life. I can take care of you and we can be together." "Naah dude," Greg announced, "you need to get to steppin.' This is my girl. I was here first." "Who are you?" Tony asked, "The delinquent boyfriend who lets his girl go to Vegas by herself? You need to get it together brother." "No, you need to check yourself!" Greg raised his voice, "I will put my foot up your ass!" Greg didn't hesitate as he came at Tony. A couple of guys grabbed Greg and restrained him as the security guard arrived telling them they had to leave the property at once. The guard escorted both men off the property. Tasha was instructed to stay inside for a moment until these guys left the premises. During the mayhem, Cynthia came down the elevator. "What happened girl?" Cynthia asked. "Greg and Tony met," Tasha told her, "and they almost got into a fight." "The sex you gave Tony must have been soooo good," Cynthia replied, "this guy is not going away. 'Houston, we have a problem.'"

After being thrown off the property at Tasha's job, Greg called Tasha. "Is Cynthia there with you?" Greg asked. "Yeah," Tasha responded. "We, the three of us, need to have a meeting!" Greg said in anger, "Let's meet at Paradise." "Ok." Tasha answered. She told Cynthia what Greg said. The girls headed over to Paradise. Once all three of them were there, they sat down in the living room. Greg started. "Ok, so I met Mr. Tony,." Greg announced, "This is going to be a problem. I don't want to go to jail behind this garbage. But I will kill him. This guy has no respect for my relationship with Tasha. He will continue to pursue Tasha no matter what..." "...Greg, slow down," Tasha stated, "we can work through this thing and no one is going to jail..." "...Greg is right," Cynthia confirmed, "this guy is not going to stop. He is obsessive and he is determined. This is how he climbed to the top of his company. Something has to be done." "Ok," Tasha added, "I will speak with him." "No way," Greg replied, "that is what he wants. To him you are the weak link. He thinks he can break you down. Since he had sex with you he thinks he owns you. He will only try to use your emotions to get back in bed with you. Tasha do not speak to him. That is not the solution." "Let me get him a girl from the club," Cynthia suggested, "we need to replace Tasha with someone else he would be interested in." "That won't work either." Greg explained, "He is rich. He can buy any girl he wants. No, he wants Tasha. She is a woman who thinks for herself and not owned or beholden to anyone. He needs an independent woman who is self-assured, self-directed and doesn't need anyone to take care of her." "They have call girls who make from 5k to 10k a day." Cynthia detailed, "These girls are trained in psychology and they know how to handle a man like Tony." "No," Greg voiced, "he can pay any price for a prostitute. The man is loaded. No Cynthia, that is not what he needs. He needs someone like you." "Me?" Cynthia spoke in disbelief. "You are exactly the type of woman that Tony respects." Greg explained, "He knows you don't need him, you are independent, and you are a power house. He could fall for you." Rose was listening to the conversation. Before Cynthia or Tasha could respond to what Greg was suggesting, she interjected herself into the conversation. "I apologize, but I couldn't help but overhear what you all were discussing," Rose interrupted, "Cynthia has something very powerful she could offer Tony. Something Tony would not be able to ignore." "What's that Mrs. Rose?" Greg curiously asked. "Her business," Rose specified, "Cynthia could offer a merger 50-50 to Tony. He would be completely obligated to strongly consider it because it will solve all his problems and make both parties very, very rich." "What?" Cynthia asked genuinely surprised. "Do you think I would give this fool my company? There is no way Ma. I worked too hard to build this company." "Yeah, it's time for someone else to do the work," Rose told Cynthia, "Tony is driven. If you merged with his company, he would take the new company even higher. Even further than you can imagine. I've watched him for years. He is a man possessed." "Cynthia, you got Tasha into this mess." Greg reminded her, "It seems to me, if you really are a friend to Tasha, you would be willing to help her get out of this situation. What do you think Cynthia?" "Greg, I don't know." Cynthia shared, "I haven't given it any thought." "Ok, that's true," Greg reasoned, "let's brainstorm this together right now for the first time." "Well, in order to distract this guy's attention away from Tasha," Cynthia reasoned out loud thoughtfully, "I would have to understand why he likes Tasha. He hasn't even known her for a full week yet, so his connection to Tasha is truly weak at this point. From a psychological standpoint, Tony is really vulnerable right now. If I were to act it would need to be sooner rather than later." "So, how would you go about getting this hyper-alpha male's attention Cynthia?" Greg asked. "You want me to tell you all of my secrets Greg?" Cynthia questioned with a smile. "No, it's simple. You give him what he can't resist." "I'm scared to ask what that is." Greg commented smiling. "I can't offer him a relationship because he hates me." Cynthia expressed, "I can't offer him other women because he already has that. I can only offer him the one thing I know he wants Greg. This guy would love to fuck me. I see it in his eyes every time we have a corporate meeting with his firm. He would love to brag and say 'I banged Cynthia Heart,' to his board of directors. God Greg, I can't give him that honor. I can't offer him that prize, even I have my pride. I have limitations. I can't do it, but I do know how to do it." "What did Tasha give up helping you break into Tony's safe?" Greg released strategically. "Oh Greg," Cynthia replied, "you are good. You are showing me I would be the biggest hypocrite because Tasha gave this man her sex; her best sex to help me. She damn near sacrificed her treasured relationship with her man to benefit my company. Ahhhh, you are very, very clever Greg." "It's the truth," Greg told her, "it's not clever. It's what actually happened. Cynthia, will you do this for both of us?" "Ok, I will think about it," Cynthia said, "but if I do it, I need to pick Tasha's mind. I need to know everything that happened between her and Tony. So, girlfriend you are staying here at Paradise with me for the time being. You will help me plan 'The Seduction Of Tony.' And Greg, you are not off the hook either. We will talk later."

Cynthia knew if she was going to do this, she had to strike soon. Maybe in two days or so, no longer. She had connections at the agency where Tony ordered his call girls. She wanted to know what kind of girls he liked and with enough money, you can retrieve this information. She found out his favorite color, his favorite type of girl, the kind of lingerie he preferred, and what were his favorite sexual positions. She made poor Tasha go through every position he put her in, how he did it to her, what he said, and why he did what he did. The 'why' was the most important thing. Cynthia became a woman possessed. Actually, she was enjoying planning this thing. Tasha could really see her getting into it. Cynthia was like a big sister to her, and now Cynthia was getting her out of trouble.

Priscilla may be out of Greg's life, but he was still on her mind. Priscilla didn't trust Cynthia, and she thought Cynthia might ruin Greg and Tasha. She decided to become a detective and track down information about Cynthia. Again, she could lose her job over this if she was caught, but even more importantly, something could happen to Greg and Tasha if she didn't do this research. Here is what Priscilla wanted to know: why a person who is a billionaire is working a 9-5 for 60k? (It makes no sense.), and what is her fascination with Greg? He's a nice enough guy, but she could have any man who she wants. Therefore, Priscilla hired a private eye. His name is Ben Jackson. He had connections all over town and was really good with a computer. He charged $125 a day. You didn't have to pay him if he didn't get results which was different from other private detectives. This is why Priscilla hired him. After 3 days he acquired Cynthia's work history. Now Priscilla knew the jobs she worked before she started working with Tasha. She casually visited Cynthia's previous job and started noticing the various people who worked there. She'd walk behind them on the sly and try to listen to their conversations. Priscilla noticed the attractive receptionist, who was always sitting at the front desk. The receptionist knew everyone at the job and kept her finger on the pulse of what was going on. Priscilla approached the girl one day after work and struck up a conversation with her. Priscilla asked her about the job, what kind of business this was, and also the salary like she was looking for a job. The receptionist's name was

Rachel. Rachel informed Priscilla to come back tomorrow and get an application. She did, but she waited until the end of the day. The girl gave her the application and was getting ready to leave work. Priscilla walked with her to her car talking. She asked her if she ever heard of a woman name Cynthia Heart. Rachel replied, "Yeah, why are you asking?" "Honestly, she is causing a lot of trouble for my friend." Priscilla replied truthfully. "This girl was a mess." Rachel informed, "She nearly destroyed the relationship of two of our workers." "Can I get your number and call you later when you have time to talk?" Priscilla asked, "Because I need to know so I can help my friend." The two exchanged numbers and Priscilla set up a time to call her. Rachel proved to be a treasure trove of valuable information. She told a very similar story to what was happening between Greg and Tasha. Over the phone, Rachel explained to Priscilla that Cynthia befriended one of the young ladies at that job. The lady's name was Trina. She was beautiful and seeing a guy named Doug. Doug was a handsome, good guy, well raised, and he really loved Trina. They were the perfect couple. She introduced the idea of having a threesome before you get married. Somehow, she convinced Trina to try it. Well, needless to say, it wrecked their relationship. It was a complete disaster. Priscilla could see this was a pattern. This is the reason the billionaire Cynthia works 40 hours a week. She is pretending to be just like everyone else to gain the trust of some unsuspecting coworker with an attractive boyfriend.

Priscilla figured it out. Now she just needed to inform Greg before it was too late. Priscilla decided to write an anonymous letter. She would not add her name so she wouldn't lose her job if Cynthia ever came across the letter. She would use a symbol, a heart with a diamond in it. Greg would know who wrote the letter. Priscilla explained Cynthia's pattern of destroying relationships by befriending coworkers and sleeping with their handsome boyfriends under the pretext of a threesome. She placed the letter in Greg's door one morning right before he would leave for work. She knew his schedule and daily routine. Priscilla stood around the corner, out of sight, to make sure he received the letter. The heart symbol was on the outside of the envelope. There was a message on the back of the envelope telling Greg to destroy the envelope. This way it was impossible to trace it back to Priscilla. With the message in Greg's hand, her job was done.

After reading the letter Greg knew he had to show it to Tasha. The information Priscilla shared was priceless. It helped to explain so much about Cynthia. However, at this point, with Cynthia trying to seduce Tony, and possibly merging her company with his, this previous narrative was changing. Cynthia, if she succeeds, will become the hero. She will save Tasha and Greg's relationship, and eliminate the threesome. She will make herself a much richer woman than she already is and she will get a man of her own; not her girlfriend's man. Cynthia will have her own man, and if all goes well, they will get married.

Greg and Tasha were working through their problems little by little. Greg's business was growing and he needed to hire help. He called Angel and asked if she was still interested in working during the day. She could do 3 days a week. Greg found another person to work with her during the day. He paid them according to how well they performed. The better they were at their job, the more money they could make. It was a system which seemed to work out well for everyone. Greg purchased a lot of his food for his business from a local grocery store. The young man who helped him with his large meat orders was named Trevor. Trevor was a very sharp polite guy with a pretty good sense of humor. He was also a Philadelphia Eagles fan who used to live in Pennsylvania. Greg and Trevor talked about football a lot. A thought hit Greg. This would be a good guy for Priscilla. He was young, polite, and principled. Greg started taking time to get to know him better. Greg would probe him every time he had the chance, asking him questions about his upbringing, and his views on life. One day Greg asked him about his goals. He said he wanted to start his own business one day. He wanted to work for himself.

The Eagles were going to play Dallas Sunday. Greg invited Trevor over for the game. Trevor made a request, "I will come if you cook those tasty wings from your food truck." "Ok, that's a deal." Greg responded, "See you Sunday." The more time Greg spent with Trevor, the more he realized this was a quality guy. Tasha also liked him. She said he was compassionate, honest, and insightful. Yeah, Greg felt confident this was the guy for Priscilla. The only problem would be convincing Trevor that Priscilla was a quality girl because she worked at a strip club. Greg didn't know how to explain her to Trevor, but he knew it wouldn't be easy.

However, Greg had an idea. He would send a letter to Priscilla and ask her how he should proceed. Greg asked Angel to get Priscilla's home address. She got it for Greg with no problems. Greg wrote a letter to Priscilla expressing how he met a nice young man he wanted her to meet. Priscilla responded in a letter, leaving at his front door again. She was informing Greg to tell the young man she would call him when he's available on the weekend. Greg received Trevor's number and sent it to Priscilla notifying her to call any time after 12 this Saturday.

Cynthia wanted to talk to Greg. She called him. "Greg, how are you?" Cynthia asked. "I'm good." Greg answered. "You know in order for me to do this," Cynthia commented, "you are going to have to make love to me one last time." "I kinda figured something like that." Greg responded. "Come by Paradise tonight." Cynthia said. When Greg arrived, Cynthia opened the door wearing a beautiful robe. There were no words spoken. She smiled and grabbed his hand leading him to her bedroom on the first floor. "This is the very last time you will make love to me Greg." Cynthia emphasized, "Make it count." She sat Greg down on the bed and went into the bathroom. She came out just a few moments later. "Oh, my, my, my." Greg muttered under his breath. She was wearing the exact same outfit she had on at Tasha's place when they first started the threesome. It was the red lingerie outfit which didn't cover the breasts or the coochie. And of course, to make it perfectly authentic, Cynthia had a dab of whipped cream over both nipples and some covering her coochie. "That is exactly what you said the first night you really made love to me." Cynthia reminded him. "And do you remember your first words that night?" Greg asked. "Hello, Greg," Cynthia said sweetly, "I'm Delicious, pleased to meet you." They both laughed as they reminisced on that special moment in their relationship. "Could you taste me to make sure I'm really Delicious?" Cynthia asked mimicking the first time. "Don't mind if I do." Greg played along. "Delicious, there are certain things that you can never forget." Greg took his time, he started with her nipples, licking them clean, tasting them and squeezing her breasts. She went back in time to the beginning. That was the night that Cynthia Heart fell in love with Greg. Greg was on his knees tasting her deliciousness. He was in no rush; he was recreating the most passionate encounter between the both of them. They went back to a time when nothing else mattered at that moment. Greg had completely forgot about Tasha and Cynthia was falling for Greg all the way. That night Greg became her King, her Master. Cynthia pulled Greg up and began to kiss him tenderly. "Oh my, orange flavored kisses, just like the first time." Greg said really surprised that Cynthia remembered the most intimate details, she never forgot that night. That made Greg feel like he was truly her man, her King. Cynthia pushed Greg so that he sat down on the edge of the bed. She kneeled before him like he was royalty. Maintaining eye contact she went for his tool. Cynthia put it in her warm wet mouth slowly. It felt so good to Greg. Now he remembered exactly what happened on that fateful Friday night. Cynthia had outdone herself. She was recreating the night Greg let loose and made real love to her. She recreated it perfectly. Greg was moaning softly as she continued to please him with her warm mouth. The love making continued. Cynthia pushed Greg to the center of her bed. She climbed up on him, straddling him, making his manhood slide right up inside of her. She began to work her hips. It felt so good to Greg. And guess what Cynthia asked? "...And I am your heart?" She asked slowly pleasuring him. "And you are my heart." Greg repeated faithfully. "And I am Delicious?" She inquired sweetly continuing to rotate her hips while riding him. "And you are very Delicious." Greg answered. "And you will never hurt me?" Cynthia asked. "And Cynthia Heart, I will never hurt you." He said smiling and remembering. "Cynt, I must have been crazy to commit to a promise before hearing it." Greg told her reminiscing. "It's called trust baby." Cynthia replied. "It's why you opened up." Cynthia kept working her hips. Greg knew he would eventually cum if she didn't slow down. So Greg took control. He flipped her on her back and took her ankles putting them over his shoulders. It was time to take Cynthia to heaven. "Oh my Greg," Cynthia uttered with excitement, "are you doing to me what you did to Tatianna? I heard the story." "You just sit back and relax Delicious." Greg started thrusting trying to find the correct angle. All Cynthia could do was wait. Greg was in total control. "Ahhhh," Cynthia moaned, "Ohhhh. She continued to sigh and moan. Greg was almost there. "I ... want ... you ... to ... feel ... this ..." With his last thrust Cynthia climaxed inside. Her whole body trembled. She reached a strong orgasm on Greg's command. After all, he was her Prince, and her King. Cynthia clung to her man with all her might. "Oh my God that felt so good Greg. How am I supposed to make love to Tony after a performance like that?" "I promise Delicious, you will do fine like you always do. Thank you Precious for this wonderful walk down memory lane. It was truly special. Now don't you ever forget this night."

Priscilla and Trevor were getting to know one another over the phone. They called each other on a regular basis. They talked about any and everything. Trevor was becoming a very good friend to Priscilla. She didn't tell him she was a stripper yet. This information would come soon enough. However, she did share she wanted to create another stream of income whether it was from investing, or from starting a small business. Of course, this was right up Trevor's alley. Priscilla shared she had a little money saved and was willing to invest in a small business. They brainstormed together and decided to do the same business Greg was doing selling wings and dinners off of a food truck. The reason this was their choice is because Priscilla worked on Greg's food truck. She had experience in his business and because Trevor worked at the grocery store in the meat department. These two elements went hand in hand. Priscilla put a down payment on a food truck and their business was off to a wonderful start. Priscilla would work during the day and Trevor would work after 5 pm. They operated their truck on a different side of town as not to compete with Greg. The city was very big and there were so many people that it really didn't matter. Little by little their business started to become profitable. After two months it was time to hire a worker to help out.

Priscilla was great with the paper work and all the official things needed to be done. Trevor, on the other hand, was a huge success with the customers and generating new business. Trevor spoke with Greg a lot to get his advice, and input, which he found invaluable. (Trevor and Prescilla pic below.)

Priscilla realized the time had come to finally tell Trevor what she did for a living. Their relationship was sufficiently strong. He knew who she was as a person. He saw her hard work, her dedication, and devotion. Trevor knew all of her good traits so Priscilla thought it was time to let him know. She wanted to talk to him face to face. She invited him to a quiet little restaurant where they could talk. She explained the way their business was going that she should be able to quit her job in a few months, but she needed to tell him first. "Trevor, I work at a strip club." Priscilla informed him with butterflies in her stomach, "I've been a stripper for 2 years now." "R e a l l y...?" Trevor replied slowly thinking, "...You are stunningly beautiful Priscilla..., so that makes sense..., but you don't have to do that kind of work. It is degrading and you are so much better than that." Well, Priscilla was relieved. This was a better response than she expected. However, the question that was on her mind was, 'Does this disqualify me from being your girl?' "Trevor, I did this to support my son and my mom." Priscilla expressed, "At the time I had no idea about investing or starting my own business. I didn't have a clue. I never had a financial education. Someone just recently put the thought in my head that I could take my money and invest it in a business. I make no excuses for stripping. I'm just telling you what happened to me. I want you to hear it from me and I want you to understand. Stripping is not who I am, it is what I do for now." "You make a lot of money..., don't you?" Trevor asked, "That's why you had the money to put down on the truck..., right? But Priscilla, we can take this and make it something wonderful. I want to get you out of that life and be financially independent. You know Priscilla, it's about time we started thinking about taking some of our profit to get another truck and another employee..."

This conversation with Trevor made Priscilla's heart burst with joy. He didn't condemn her or accuse her. This was a very good start. He still accepted her as his business partner and Trevor wants to expand the business. Priscilla was determined to make this business a total success. She got to work on planning how to expand the business. Two months later Priscilla left he strip club for the very last time. Trevor threw her a big party, and everyone thought the party was about the recent expansion of their business; adding another truck. Not at all. It was really about his beautiful girl friend getting out the strip club, getting out of the stripping business, and becoming a successful self-made co-owner of a small business. A business which was growing. Trevor gave Priscilla something to work for at the party. He took her to the side and told her his vision for the company. "I think we can add another truck in a couple of months to cover the southside." Trevor detailed, "When we get our third truck, we will start saving all of our profits for a period of time. We will put expansion on hold for about 6-8 months. According to my calculations, then we will be ready." "Ready for what?" Priscilla asked, "Ready for what?" "Ready for something wonderful and big." Trevor promised, "Just trust me. it will be a welcomed surprise. So, let's just get to work."

Meanwhile, as Priscilla and Trevor were doing their thing, Cynthia tried to get Tony off Tasha's back. She was ready to go and she had a plan. This was something she knew she had to do by herself. Tasha could not be around her, and Greg definitely couldn't be around either. Cynthia was on her own for this mission. She called Tony. "It's Cynthia Heart." She addressed and asked, "You still in town?" "Cynthia Heart," Tony replied, "Yes I'm still in town." "I'd like to meet with you." Cynthia stated, "I have a business proposal you really need to consider." "Is this a trick?" Tony asked, "You're not going to try to kidnap me or something?" He laughed. "Ok, where shall we meet?" Tony questioned. "Meet me in one hour at the Waldorf Astoria. Inside the restaurant Brassica in Buckhead." Cynthia answered. "Yes, I know the place." Tony replied. "Drinks are on me." Cynthia offered.

Cynthia arrived first and acquired a table. "Yes, I'm expecting a gentleman by the name of Tony. He should be arriving shortly." Cynthia noted to the hostess. She was slightly nervous though she had no reason to be. Cynthia was wearing a grey suit jacket with a red skirt that came to the middle of her thighs. She looked very professional like she was attending a business meeting, which of course she was. Before Cynthia left for this meeting with Tony, Greg gave her some last-minute instructions. "Cynthia, this is your moment." Greg encouraged her, "You are about to make history with this proposed merger of two super-powerful companies. They won't see this thing coming. You are going to catch the world by surprise." "Greg, I'm offering this man sex." Cynthia replied, "I feel like a high-class call girl." "No, stop thinking this way." Greg specified, "You are a powerful business owner who has come up with a brilliant idea no one has even considered. You are outside of the box. Tony will be completely caught off guard Cynt. You have the power coupled with the element of surprise. This is a chess match, and you have already considered all the possible moves after deep analysis." "Greg, the only thing is I'm scared." She responded, "I have to be vulnerable to pull this off. I have to let my archenemy screw me. I'm a woman in a man's world." "Yeah," Greg continued, "you've never let that stop you before. In fact, it was fuel for your fire. Remember anything they can do, you can do better, right? Now is your time to be a woman. Think of it like this. If you are going to allow a man to share in the leadership of your company, don't you need to test him? Don't you need to know what kind of leader he is? Is he man enough to lead you or your company? Do you trust this guy? Is he a great decision maker? What better way than to find out up close and personal? How does he make love to a woman? Does he fuck her? Or does he take his time to learn her and lead her? Today you will find out what kind of man Tony really is. Is this guy man enough to lead you and your company?" "Wow, I didn't think of it like this." Cynthia reasoned out loud, "I should treat this like an interview for a job. Right? Then I shouldn't be nervous. He should be nervous. It's not me having sex with him. It's Tony having sex with me. I can put the pressure on him and remove it from me. He has the most to lose not me. He has to show me who he is. Is he man enough to lead me? I'm so glad we had this talk Greg. You are the best." "Go give him hell!!!" Greg boldly enforced, "You were born to do this! You were born for a moment like this! Cynthia you will do fine. Just relax and be you, be bold, and be bad." Greg smiled at her.

Cynthia remembered this pep talk when she looked up and saw Tony making his way to their table. "Hey Tony." Cynthia started off. "Ms. Heart. Hello." Tony replied. "I want to run something pass you." Cynthia continued, "What if we could eliminate the conflict between our companies? What if we could raise the white flag and stop fighting each other? Do you think this would be good for both of our companies?" "Sure," Tony thoughtfully voiced, "we could literally save millions of dollars and spend that money on research and development, or on expanding our reach and our product line. Absolutely, this would be great." "Well, in order to do this, you and I would have to work closely together as the respective CEOs of these two companies." Cynthia catalogued, "Do you think we are capable of working together Tony? Billions upon billions of dollars are at stake." "Wow, honestly Ms. Heart, I never even thought along these lines before." Tony disclosed, "You are catching me completely off guard here, and that is saying something. If I'm understanding what you are proposing, I owe it to my employees, my board of directors, and to the shareholders to consider this possibility. And of course, I am a professional. I can work with you despite our long history of being archenemies." "Well Tony, you may be a bigger man than I thought you were." Cynthia directed. "What I'm proposing clear and simple is a merger. 50-50 of our companies." She stopped and looked Tony dead in his eyes waiting for his reaction. "Hmmm, you are serious." Tony said with focused thought, "This is not some kind of corporate trap where I lose my company in the end?" "Your problem is you don't trust me." She described, "You think I'm playing some kind of game here." "Ms. Heart," Tony stated in a professional tone, "you must understand this is a complete reversal and change in direction one hundred eighty degrees in a split second. Remember, just about a week ago you were stealing information from my safe. Now you want to play nice and merge our companies together. You can see how this is hard to believe. You have to agree with my position." "Yeah Tony," Cynthia replied, "you are right. This is sudden and totally against the grain. However, it is a good thing if we can make this happen. I guess what we need here is to start off with a little trust. In fact, let's just start over." Cynthia stood up from the table and started walking to the door. She stopped and turned around. Tony was trying to figure out what was going on. She returned to the table. "Hello, my name is Cynthia Heart," She reintroduced herself and asked, "and you?" "I'm Tony," He responded smiling, "pleased to meet you." "Tony, I want to make you a proposition today." Cynthia announced as she sat down again, "Would you like to have sex with me? If you can show me that you are a man deserving to be followed, I will give you my company. We can merge our businesses." "What!? Tony exclaimed stupefied, "What are you saying?" "I'm interviewing you for a job." Cynthia delegated, "Are you a man? A leader? Someone worthy of me following? Tony, I can tell a lot by the way a man has sex. Some men can lead a woman and some men just know how to stick it in a woman. I'm not giving my company over to a man who is not worthy. I'm already rich Tony. Money is no problem for me. I don't need anyone to take care of me. I'm good. Therefore, if I merge with you, I have to have a reason. I have to trust your leadership, your decision making, and your judgment. Tony, show me you are a man; a real man. Show me you are the leader I'm looking for. The leader I have been looking for all of my life. Make love to me and I will be the judge of what kind of man that you are. This is between you and I Tony. This is a onetime offer. Are you man enough to take my challenge?" Cynthia stood up again and walked over to Tony's side of the table. She innocently articulated, "Could you help me take off my jacket?" Tony helped her remove her jacket. As Cynthia turned around to sit back down, Tony could not believe his eyes. She had on white suspenders. Two strips of white thin cloth that came over her shoulders and connected to her skirt at the waist. Each of the white strips of cloth split her titties in half covering only the nipples. They barely covered her delicious breasts which swayed each time she moved. You could see a faint outline of her perky nipples through the thin white material which the suspenders were made from. This outfit was sexually explicit and erotically shocking. It most certainly caught Tony's attention as it was designed to do. Tony's eyes were fixated on her sweet tender breasts. She knew that was one of his weaknesses. Cynthia paused letting Tony be completely engulfed in this moment. She made them jiggle just a little for him as she repositioned herself in her chair with a devilish over confident smile. Cynthia did not interrupt his viewing pleasure. Tony had fallen into a trance. He was temporarily hypnotized and totally enchanted by her titillating breasts. Cynthia thought to herself, 'Sometimes it's good to be bad.' "...So..., ...are you man enough to take my challenge?" Cynthia asked after a sustained pause. "...Yes I am," Tony responded waking up from his trance. He understood exactly what Cynthia was saying and exactly what Cynthia was offering. "When do you want to do this?" "Now. Right now Tony." She answered, "I hope you are ready?" "Oh I'm ready." Tony smoothly said with confidence as he pulled out his cell phone and dialed a number. "Yes, this is Tony. Do you have an Astoria King Suite available right now? No, I don't want a regular suite. I want the King Suite. Ok, then I will be over to get the key to the room presently. Thank you." Tony got up from the table and told Cynthia to wait until he returned with the key card for the Astoria King Suite. His eyes were still panning over her tasty breasts.

Cynthia waited patiently until he returned. He put his arm out, she stood up, and grabbed his arm. He escorted Cynthia to the elevator like a perfect gentleman. Once they reached the suite, Tony went to the shower turning it on. He took control of everything. Cynthia didn't have to say or do a thing. Tony led her to the bathroom and began to take off her clothes like she was his girlfriend of a long time. The warm water of the shower felt so good on Cynthia's naked curvy body, but Tony's hands felt even better. He was rubbing her neck and massaging her shoulders with the soapy water streaming down her body dripping off her voluptuous breasts. Cynthia was aroused. It was unbelievable to be intimate with someone you have always fought against; your enemy. How could she be trusting him now with her most precious body? This was new territory. For the first time since forever Cynthia had her own man. He was not the boyfriend of her girlfriend. Tony was all hers. It was a strange feeling, but a very good wholesome feeling.

She wanted to go at Tony. She wanted to please him, but she remembered tonight was Tony's chance to please her, to lead her. He had to show Cynthia he was worthy of her and worthy of her business. This encounter was all about his leadership. He dried Cynthia's beautiful body off and led her to the bed. Tony looked back at Cynthia's beautiful perky breasts as they bounced and swayed with each step. They captivated him. He couldn't help it. Tony pulled the covers all the way back making room for her on the king-sized bed. He began by massaging her breasts with oil. Tony was in no rush. He wanted to show her she could trust him and he was fully committed. She knew he was fascinated with her breasts, but she was about to detonate in pleasure. She was getting very very wet. Cynthia wanted him to put his ample manhood inside of her. She could see that he was erect. He was ready and she was ready too, but Tony started to go down on Cynthia. He began to kiss her neck, her breasts, and her stomach. He was working his way down getting ever closer to her sweet essence. "Mmmmm..., that feels so good Tony," She released in pleasure, "Don't stop, don't stop." "As you wish Ms. Heart." Tony replied getting back to his assignment. Cynthia was realizing this guy was a man motivated. Why she never thought of making him her ally is crazy. What a great idea she thought now that she was in bed with him; literally in bed with him. Tony was making Cynthia want it. Her clit was throbbing by this time, and now Tony was ready to make his move. With Cynthia laying on her back, he hovered over her putting his weight on his elbows. He positioned himself to slide right inside her warm wet treasure. He slipped in effortlessly, and now she began to feel his rhythm. He was setting the pace and her heart began to beat harder and faster. She loved his attention to detail, his patience, and his deliberate steady penetration. Cynthia had her eyes closed. She was truly enjoying this experience, but when she opened her eyes, she could see Tony staring at her. She knew what he was doing. He was trying to gauge her reaction to the way he was making love to her. Tony wanted to see what pleased her the most. He altered his stroke and watched to see if she moaned or gave some other indication that she liked what he was doing; or even how much she liked what he was doing. Cynthia wanted to get into this game. Tony proved he could love her like a man and that he could take the lead. However, Cynthia knew love was a two way street. She had held back long enough. It was time for her to give it to him. "Babe...," She sighed, "let me..." Cynthia directed him to roll onto his back. She climbed up on top sliding him inside of her cowgirl style, her favorite position. "Mmmm," Tony moaned as Cynthia started her hips in motion. She was facing him working it back and forth slowly. This time she was looking at him. Her titties were rocking back and forth with the swaying of her hips. Cynthia started to pick up the pace a little and asked him, "You like that?" "Oh yeah..., oh yeah..." Tony murmured breathing in between the rocking of her hips. "You know Tony," She whispered clearly, "I'm very powerful up here." "Mmhmm." was all he could say. "I'm riding one of the richest black men in the U.S." Cynthia boasted, "And what's more? I know he is totally enjoying it, and it won't be my last time. It's actually my first time. Tony, I have a confession to make." Cynthia admitted as she starting going round and round with her hips changing the rhythm, "I've never really had a man since college. I mean my own man. I just borrowed some beautiful girl's boyfriend from time to time. I've never managed to keep him though. But I got some good sex out of the deal." "Really?" Tony asked feeling surprised not just by what she revealed, but he was surprised she shared such an intimate truth about herself with him. "Yeah, but I like this better." She confessed, "It makes more sense for me to go out and get my own man. This way I can pick the best man and I can build a permanent relationship no one can break up." "Hmmm, so you want a permanent relationship?" Tony asked very interested in her response. "Yes," Cynthia answered without hesitation, "and I want this relationship with you. The best man I've ever seen in my life. The best man for me." "Good." Is all Tony said like he was waiting for that cue. He rolled Cynthia on her back and re-entered her with a passion never before seen by Cynthia. He rhythmically started thrusting deep inside of her. "I... will... never... leave... you..." Tony promised as he methodically penetrated his precious new lover. "Now you say it to me. You say it to me." "Oh... I... will... never... leave... you..." Cynthia uttered in perfect synchronicity to his deep penetrating thrusts. "That is our commitment to each other Ms. Heart." Tony assured her, "If this is what you want, this is what I promise you and what I will commit to." "Oh my God Tony." She asked, "What have we done here?" "Ms. Heart," he replied, "we just merged our companies, but more importantly, we have just merged our lives together forever." "Then this calls for a celebration." Cynthia responded, "A private intimate celebration of pleasure." She started kissing her way down his body. She wanted to please her man. She finally arrived below his waist. She stuffed the head of it right into her mouth and sucked it well savoring his erection. "You are sooooo good at that." Tony says submerged in ecstasy. "Lucky for you I am." Cynthia boasted. There was no more talking for a while. Tony just leaned back on his arms and let Cynthia do her thing, or should we say let Cynthia do her private celebration thing. This is one celebration Tony will not soon forget.

When Tony returned to his corporate headquarters in Charlotte, NC, he was not alone. There was a board meeting at 10:30am. It was time for the big announcement. The lawyers from both businesses had already met and ironed out the details. No one on the board had any idea what was about to happen. Cynthia sat quietly outside the room where they were having the meeting. Tony opened up the meeting and welcomed everyone. "Today is a day that will go down in history for Tru-Max." Tony announced, "We are going to solve one of our biggest problems, and position this company to attain limitless profits at the same time!" He smiled as he looked around the room and made a dramatic pause. "…Let our guest in please." The door opened and Cynthia Heart entered the room. Every member of the board gasped, and there were a couple which protested. "Come on Tony! She should be arrested!" One of the board members uttered agitated. "Wait, wait, wait, calm down."

Tony told everyone, "Let's hear her out." "Hello, my name is Cynthia Heart," She started out, "I came to Tony last week and proposed something impossible. Something incredible. I proposed that we merge our companies, stop fighting, and start making more money together. With the combined resources of both of our powerful companies, we can move forward and move forward quickly." "I didn't know if I should take her seriously," Tony admitted, "because of the previous week, she was accused of stealing secrets from us. However, I decided to hear her out, and I'm glad I did. The lawyers from both companies have worked out the details. This is a legitimate offer and both sides are protected. We have nothing to lose." "So gentlemen," Cynthia declared, "today we will sign the final papers, and Cynthia Heart will no longer be your enemy. She will become your best and most cherished ally." Cynthia took a pen and signed her name on the document. Tony took his pen and signed the document. "It is done." Tony announced. "Now we will start working together. The board of directors from Cynthia's company will arrive here this afternoon. You are to extend the warmest welcome. Department heads will work with department heads from the other company and we will make a very smooth professional merger. A round of applause for Ms. Cynthia Heart everyone. Tony started clapping by himself at first. Then one or two others starting clapping, and gradually everyone in the meeting started clapping. The merger was finalized.

A couple of months had gone by. Priscilla and Trevor were

making progress in their business. They successfully added a third truck. Priscilla had been on Trevor to quit his job at the grocery store. He was reluctant. He told Priscilla he could probably quit the job and everything would be ok, but he wanted to keep the income from the job to pour money into their business without touching their business profits. Nevertheless, Trevor assured her he would leave his job soon because it would take a lot of pressure off Priscilla. Trevor was very goal oriented and ran a very tight business. He didn't waste time or money. Priscilla trusted his judgment, but she was getting tired.

As for Greg and Tasha, things started looking up for them as well. With Tony out of the picture, Greg and Tasha started to rebuild their relationship. The threesome was over. There were no more threats to their happiness. Tasha continued to work at her job. Greg was finally able to quit his job and replace his income with his food truck business. His business was also doing well. He was getting ready for his first expansion truck. Greg had a plan of implementation. Once he had his new truck set up and going well, he would ask for Tasha's hand in marriage. This would be about 6 months away into the future. He was already getting butterflies, but he knew she was the right girl for him. They had been through hell and high water, but they were still together.

Meanwhile Tasha, Cynthia, and Rose were busy planning a wedding. It was going to take place at Paradise in one month. Tony was footing the bill and the girls were spending like crazy. They had to plan the food, the guests, the flowers, the band, the wedding dress, and the bridesmaid's dresses. The couple was going on their honeymoon in Tahiti. Tasha was genuinely happy for her friend. She needed to settle down. This made her start thinking about her situation. When was she going to settle down?

"Greg, how old do you think is a good age to get married?" Tasha asked. "Ummm, it all depends on the person." Greg answered philosophically, "Some marry young and others have to go through a few relationships before they find the right person." "What about us?" Tasha asked a little more aggressively, "What do you think is a good age to get married? I never thought or considered Cynthia would be married before me." "Ohhhh, so that's what this is all about." Greg responded, "Your friend is getting married so you feel left out. You think it's time for you to get married, right?" "Kinda." Tasha admitted. "Well don't you worry your pretty little head about nothing," Greg promised, "your time will come. It will be here before you know it." "What are you talking about Greg?" She asked. "I'm not talking about anything," Greg answered, "you need to mind your business." "Greg, you tell me now, or I will leave you forever." Tasha replied jokingly, "You know I can't let this go." "I'll tell you my little surprise." Greg shared smirking a bit, "But, you have to give me some really good hot sex in order for me to talk." "This is blackmail!" Tasha exclaimed, "And I love it!!!" "It's like Cynthia always says, 'Sometimes it's good to be bad.'" Greg disclosed with a smile.

Trevor and Priscilla arrived at their goal. They worked hard chasing the bag out of those 3 trucks for about 8 months, and saving all of the profits after expenses. The bag was a sizable amount of cash for this young couple. So Trevor took Priscilla out to a very classy restaurant. This brother was dressed to kill. Priscilla had never seen him drip before. He was always in work clothes looking basic. Moreover, Priscilla noticed he didn't take her out much; maybe once a month. Trevor was saving his bag and stacking it. Therefore, she knew something was up when he took her to this fancy upscale place. The food was great, but Priscilla was very perceptive. Something was up. She played along keeping a close eye on Trevor. Right during the middle of the meal, Trevor confessed, "Priscilla, I have something that I want to say." "Ok, you have my attention." She says staring intently into his face, "What is it babe?" Trevor stood up and went to her side. He kneeled down on one knee and asked, "Priscilla, will you do me the honor of marrying me?" He pulled out a box and opened it. It was a beautiful diamond ring in the shape of a heart. The heart had a diamond in the middle. "Yes! Yes!" Priscilla lovingly responded, "This is the surprise, isn't it?" "Yes, this is what I've been waiting for. I had to wait until I had the bag for our wedding, our honeymoon, and a place for us to live." "Awwwww," choired everyone in the restaurant in unison and added a big round of applause. Priscilla started to cry as the sound of happiness echoed from the hands of those watching them. The soon to be married couple passionately embraced. Trevor kissed Priscilla and asked, "Now, can I meet your son?" "Yes, yes, of course." Priscilla replied through her tears of joy. Fortunately for Trevor and Priscilla, a few couples were already recording at their table at the very time Trevor stood up. They both captured the entire proposal from different angles. They approached Trevor with the wonderful news and he gladly gave them both his number to receive the videos by text message.

The sex was intense! Tasha was on top and she was determined to find out what Greg's little secret was. "Uh huh," Tasha says, "this will teach you to keep secrets from me." "Woooo baby, slow down." Greg begged, "You are going crazy tonight." "Babe, inquiring minds want to know." She questioned, "What's up? I did my part. I delivered some great sex. Didn't I?" "Yes you did," Greg admitted, "a deal is deal." He grabbed her and pulled her to him; close in his arms. "I was trying to keep this a secret," Greg started out, "but Cynthia getting married to Tony kinda messed it up. I'm in love with a very beautiful and wonderful woman. We have been through a lot together. Tasha, it's time to land this plane. It's time for me to settle down with the right girl. I've found her and I love her. I need to be able to provide for her. I have to find a place for us to live and I have to be able to support you baby. So, I was waiting until I got the second truck going. Then I was going to ask for your hand in marriage." "How soon do you think babe?" She examined. "I'm thinking in 3 months." Greg estimated. Tasha jumped up out of bed, "That doesn't give me enough time." She responded. "What are you talking about?" Greg asked confused. "We have to get the place for the reception and the wedding booked ahead of time. I need to find a dress. Do you know how much these dresses cost? How many people were you planning to invite to our wedding? With your family and my family, that's a lot of people. You know my mom has been wondering what is taking this guy so long to marry her daughter. Wait until she finds out…" Tasha blurted out. "…Tasha, Tasha, slow down baby," Greg interrupted her, "I haven't proposed or even gotten a 'Yes I will marry you' yet. You know the ring has to come first. You are under oath to tell no one, not even Cynthia about this, until I ask you and you say 'yes.' Do you understand?" "Oh you gotta be kidding me." Tasha replied being annoyed, "This is not fair. I'm about to burst right now. So we are changing the 3 months to 2 months. I'm telling you that right now." "Get back into bed with your man and relax your mind. Girl we are going to be fine." Greg instructed her, "You are going to learn a little patience." "I shouldn't give you anymore sex until you put a ring on my finger," She suggested, "I bet that will speed things up." "Get your behind in this bed." Greg said laughing.

Cynthia and Tony's wedding was ridiculously extravagant. They had everything you could ever desire at a wedding. They actually had 2 live bands. One to play the old-time classics and the other band to play modern day hits. There was a local church which had an undiscovered talent. A young lady of 18 years who had a voice like honey. Cynthia loved the way this girl sang. They paid her handsomely to sing at their wedding. It was simply amazing. Tasha was the maid of honor, which was a little awkward at first, but sufficient time had passed and everything was ok between Tasha & Tony. The food at the wedding was incredible as would be expected. Rose was a proud mom. She was so happy to see her daughter marry such a great guy. Tony and his new bride Cynthia

(Tony and Cynthia)

danced and had a great time with friends and family at their wedding. There were several people who toasted in their honor. We took so many pictures. Afterwards, they caught their flight headed to Tahiti. They had a wonderful honeymoon and created many great memories.

The next wedding was Priscilla's and Trevor's. Of course, their wedding was not as extravagant, but it was very moving, very powerful, and very lit. Priscilla's mother and her son were there. All of Trevor's family attended. Many of them travelled from Pennsylvania to see this remarkable young man get married to an incredible woman. Greg and Tasha were present, and Greg was so proud of Trevor. Trevor had built a business from the ground floor and had more trucks than Greg. Priscilla and Trevor were headed to Vegas for their honeymoon; The Venetian Hotel nonetheless.

A month or two after Priscilla and Trevor tied the knot, it was time for Tasha and Greg to do the same. Greg was really nervous the day of their wedding. He wasn't unsure. He was just so excited he became nervous. His crazy friend Nate was his best man. Nate may have been a little crazy, but he did not lack in wisdom and good judgment. Nate told Greg to calm down because he was marrying the right girl for him. Tasha's family, along with Greg's family, were present. There was a lot of home cooked dishes there. Catering is fine, but you can't beat Aunt Bessie's sweet potato pie, Uncle Joe's mouth-watering ribs, or Angie's mac and cheese (aka crack and cheese it's that addictive). You see Greg is from a family of southern cooking. They would have it no other way. Every one brought their best dish. There was melt in your mouth cornbread, and stuffing made with the best ingredients & herbs on the planet. The cakes were so soft and sweet. Everyone left with their bellies full and a couple of Styrofoam clamshell containers full of food for later. You know the drill: you can't eat it all today so take some with you.

The destination for the honeymoon remained a mystery. Greg made an announcement to everyone gathered there to share this special day. "Everyone, thank you for coming and thank you for cooking." Greg warmly expressed with gratitude, "Everyone, the food was the best I've ever tasted. You all made this day special to my new wife Tasha and I. Please don't eat all the cake. Y'all put some of it in the freezer so when we get back from our honeymoon, we can have another taste." Everyone laughed at Greg's attempt to be funny. Greg continued and made an announcement, "Everyone is wondering where we are going for our honeymoon. I'm taking Tasha out of the country." Everyone said, "Oooooohhhhhh," "We are going to Paris, France and then to the south of France, the French Riviera!" The guests erupted in cheers and clapping. Tasha was absolutely blown away! She always wanted to go to Paris. Her eyes were stretched wide and her jaw dropped to the floor. Her reaction blessed Greg, their family, and their friends. What a great wedding day this was for them and their attendees.

While on the airplane flying over the Atlantic, Tasha and Greg reminisced on their threesome experiment. "I'm just happy that we ended up back together and stronger than ever." Greg identified. "Yes, I must have been insane to agree to that ridiculous arrangement." Tasha reminisced, "Cynthia was very subtle and very convincing." They were in first class and just at that moment, a stewardess walked by. Greg stopped her and asked if they could have some Champagne knowing it was Tasha's favorite. "Yes sir." The stewardess answered politely. "One thing is for sure Tasha," Greg shared, "getting Cynthia to get Tony off our backs solved two problems. It prevented me from killing him and going to jail for the rest of my life, and it stopped Cynthia from her destructive habit of sleeping with her girlfriends' boyfriends. Now she has her own man and they have their hands full trying to run the newly merged company. Somehow through all this chaos we had a happy ending. Normally, this would not be the case. I guess we got lucky." "Yeah Greg, you're right," She had to admit, "we got lucky. And I got lucky to still be with you. Thank you for a wonderful wedding and I just want to say, I love you with all of my heart forever." The newlywed couple kissed and went on to enjoy their wonderful honeymoon in Paris.

The End (For now...)

(Greg and Tasha)

www.UnfazedPublishing.com